AF445586

# SUNBURNT

WITCH WAY SHORT #02

KIM NEXUS

*For Björn,*

*one of my best friends of over twenty years,*
*whose effervescent creativity, vivid imagination,*
*and endless capability to dream,*
*first made me jealous,*
*then made me strive,*
*now will always inspire me.*

*Go on, Noble Hero!*

# CONTENTS

# CHAPTER ONE

## A BEAUTIFUL MORNING

*Karrakii, circa 10 Human standard years prior*

The air was crisp and cold as it ruffled my feathers and caressed my beak. All I could hear were the sounds of the forest, strangely subdued at this early hour, and the desperate flapping of my wings as I pushed myself to the limit of my strength and endurance.

Even though pain started to blossom in my back, my four wings beat as one, and I climbed inexorably higher.

Up, up, up, until the greenish-yellow layer of the upper-most foliage was all I could see.

I would have loved to dance around the stray beams of orange sunlight breaking through the gently swaying mass of leaves, but that might have robbed me of the strength needed to pierce the treetop.

Maybe on the way down...

Down was always more manageable, as all I would have to do was stretch out my feathers and glide, let gravity take over.

Up, that was the struggle.

The struggle preordained in my name.

*First Female to fly in the open Sky.*

I had tried it often enough. Ever since I'd been a little fledgling, I'd wanted to scale the enormous distance, to scale the highest trees.

One could climb them. It was easier, many said.

It was for those weaklings who couldn't do it on their own.

No, I would do it like our kind was supposed to.

After uncounted changes in the leaf colors had made me a woman, a mate, the mother of three, after all that time training and striving, I would finally pierce the topmost layer and see the open sky.

Today, I would make it.

I could feel it in my tail feathers.

Only a little more.

The muscles in my back squeezed and shifted for all they were worth, and I could feel the cramp starting up. I only had a few heartbeats before I would have to relax them, or they might spasm and leave me unable to continue the life-essential movements. Before I would drop like a dead branch towards the dark, earthy part of the planet below.

"I can do it!" I rasped.

The leaves were only a few wingspans away.

"I CAN DO IT!"

With a deep breath, I stopped struggling, relaxed my back, and fell for two heartbeats, allowing my tortured limbs the tiniest measure of recuperation before I forced them back into service, beating all four blue-tipped black wings hard. At full length, all of my feathers spread out to catch as much air underneath as possible.

I punched clean through one of the gently swaying greenish-yellow canvases, then another and another.

Finally, I was through.

Orange light spilled over my body, suffocating heat and blinding brightness enveloped me as the majestic yellow sky filled my whole vision.

With a last, fretful effort, I swerved to the side and landed on the nearest leaf's stem.

Even though my body was utterly drained and destroyed, and my wings shivered uncontrollably as I folded them down, my soul soared.

I did it!

I really, truly did it!

Joyous laughter bubbled out of me, spilling all over the endless expanse that was my home. In unfiltered orange light, Father Sky held his doting watch over Mother Forest's unbroken greenery, caressing her with his light so that she might bring forth his children and shield them from the raw energy of his unbridled passion.

Children like me, who would dry out and burn up or be too weak to make their way back down if left in his unfiltered presence.

Already I could feel the heat simmering on my feathering, my eyes starting to feel dry and prickle. If I stayed much longer, I would faint and fall, like my namesake. The difference being that Mother Forest would not weep a pond for me, and no fruit tree would spring from my broken body. No, Mother Forest likely wouldn't even notice one tiny bird missing in her vast menagerie of life.

My family would notice, though. Those I was charged to protect would be left wanting.

With difficulty I tore myself away from the breathtaking sight, reached into a pouch at my belt, and retrieved the two feathers I'd kept for this occasion. The pain returned, palpable and unrelenting, as I stared at those pretty colors mixing in the soft downy hairs.

"You were so gorgeous," I murmured as I closed my eyes and gently rubbed them against my beak in a last caress, "Too gorgeous for this life, I guess..."

I stood, blinking resolutely into the brightness above. One of the low-orbit spaceports glittered in the far distance, its metal structure set against a still darkened sky.

"Please, Merciful Father," my voice sang, though I had to take a few extra breaths to keep it from breaking, "Shine upon my daughters in merciful distance, lead them safely into a new, bountiful life!"

Another deep breath, then I looked down, "Please, Loving Mother, protect them in their new life as you protect my son in this. May your shadow fall upon us all!"

Then I opened my hands, and the wind caught the feathers, carrying them off farther than my eyes could keep track of them.

A good sign.

With one last look around and a dry feeling in my throat, I slid down the leaf, opening my wings wide as soon as I cleared the foliage to ride the winds home.

# CHAPTER TWO

## THE ATTACK

THREE DAYS LATER, MY BACK STILL HURT WITH THE remnants of the exhaustive exercise.

"So I take it your mate didn't approve?!" STRAY RAY OF SUNLIGHT asked as she checked my spear.

I laughed, "Of course, he didn't. He always worries so much."

"Well, at least now that you've succeeded, you can stop this foolishness, yes?" satisfied that I'd continued to take good care of it, she handed me back my weapon.

We took to the air to start our daily training regiment. Despite her advanced years, my teacher always had an easy time outmaneuvering me. Today, the persistent twinge in my back only served to make my attempts at evasion more painful. Still, her offer to teach me had constituted an extraordinary honor. And not one I'd earned, exactly. STRAY RAY OF SUNLIGHT had offered me her teacher's ring because of something my father had done for her in the past. Something which everyone in our village seemed in agreement should never be discussed.

Maybe, because it happened before they settled here, when they'd fought among the stars for money, only to find that money held an empty promise, that the real joy came from flying free.

At least, that's what father had often claimed. It was a common enough sentiment amongst our people. Wings didn't work in small spaces, without gravity and air currents. Which was why, even though our people had been turned into a spacefaring species by our former masters, most would rather listen to that deep-seated, instinctual need than go off-planet. The sudden freedom from forced migration to the stars only some generations ago had sparked a new appreciation for the time before. Traditional settlements like this one had always prevailed. The old way, the wild way, had always prevailed. But now, 95 % of my people were living like our forefathers once more, in contrast to the 70 % only 30 rotations prior.

This life was all I knew, and I had no interest in the stars. I had no interest in the large settlements, which were too choked with living spaces and dead vegetation to afford their inhabitants much room to fly. Having been to one with my parents, I'd seen the spark in my father's eyes, how they followed the shuttles upward. I'd seen the spark take root in my mother too.

Who knew what father had found up there that made him yearn for the stars. He could never explain it.

STRAY RAY OF SUNLIGHT couldn't tell me either. Like she never told me what had happened between father and her.

And when I'd taken her teacher's ring and scratched my name upon it, it was understood that I would never ask about it again.

Which hadn't kept me from trying to puzzle it out on my own, of course. But since my parents had long since moved on, there were few clues to be found.

"Well...," I barely evaded the thrust of her spear, rolling in midair to gain a better position.

"You want to do it again? Go beyond the trees?" she easily side-flapped my slash, doing that thing where her form almost seemed to float backward. She'd explained the technique, and I'd tried to get it right for days on end, but my wings always tripped each other up.

But then, there was a reason why she was the master.

"Wouldn't you?"

She only cocked her head at that, her large black eyes alight with curiosity.

She didn't get it. None of them did.

Finally, she laughed, "Oh, FIRST FEMALE TO FLY IN THE OPEN SKY, you really are as crazy as your father sometimes."

Before I could form a reply, the alarm bells started ringing.

One at first, then a second, then a third. Momentarily, all of them joined the frantic choir.

Cries of rage and fear echoed through the trees and made a swarm of shadow bumbles lounging leisurely on a nearby stump take off in sudden haste.

"Raiders!" STRAY RAY OF SUNLIGHT motioned for the warriors to form groups and hurry to their assigned posts. Before she could finish her orders, a flash of light raced through the air. It punched clean through her chest and travelled on. Another student's wing was hit, and the sudden pain made him crash into a nearby tree.

"Mistress!" I dove in to help, but I knew it was too late. The light in my teacher's eyes dimmed instantly as her body stiffened, before it immediately slackened and fell.

So I turned midair to see the source of the shot. My hand threw the spear before I'd fully realized a target. Still, it hit home, and the mummed haslaroid figure cried out as I speared it through the torso, pinning it against the bark.

More lights started flashing everywhere, like condensation rain, but from all sides, not just up.

I dipped down and ripped my teacher's spear from her claw before it could accompany her down into the shadows. Under normal circumstances, I would have caught and eased her down onto a nearby branch, but there was no time.

Dishonorable as my conduct might have been, the raiders' aggressiveness could only mean one thing: They were here for the chicks, and they would take no other prisoners.

It was rare but not unheard of.

While villages all around the planet lived in fear of slavers, most would only try to sneak in and take one or two prisoners, mostly unattended chicks or lonely individuals that had wandered off too far from the protection of the group. And it didn't happen all that often.

To have well-armed troops raid a whole village and kill indiscriminately was only heard of a handful of times in recent history.

Still, the proof of what was happening lay in the desperate cries of those dropping wounded or dead all around me. Enemies surrounded us, and except for the one I'd killed, they were well hidden in the foliage. Getting to them took too long, and my brethren were slaughtered when they tried. So I didn't. I dropped like I was hit, spiraling, moving my wings around to cover my vitals. Some random beams flew my way, and two of them singed my legs, but I refused to cry out.

Once I'd cleared the immediate fighting zone, I saw the nets. I saw the bodies of my friends entangled in the dark mesh. One cowardly raider sat on a perch and shot those still moving with detached precision while another covered it. So they would take us for our feathers, too, would they?

Filthy scum!

I grabbed a tree pearl, and it broke from the bark almost soundlessly.

The first haslaroid was looking the other way, concentrated on WHISPER ON THE WIND, a ferocious warrior of the second level, who was still struggling, trying to rip the net, despite sporting several deadly wounds. Another shot left the creature's weapon just as the tree pearl left my hand to hurtle its way.

It hit its head with a resounding *whack*, and the figure dropped from its perch.

With a surprised yelp, the second one turned around in time to meet my teacher's spear with its torso. Strange sounds emerged from its mouth. Probably curses.

I shoved it off the ledge, holding fast to its weapon and mine.

As I studied the object, it quickly became apparent that I wouldn't be able to use it. What seemed to be the firing mechanism was half-hidden inside a flat metal tube, which my fingers were too large to enter. So I cast the thing into the shadows too.

WHISPER ON THE WIND wasn't moving anymore; no one was.

I jumped off the ledge and circled the open space. My teacher's spear was well-sharpened and made short work of the nets' suspension points. Better to have the dead fall into the shadows than have them desecrated by these filthy strangers!

"MOTHER! FATHER!" the cries of the young clung to the breeze.

Angry shouting and calls to attack accompanied them, but the males were quickly silenced, and only the fledglings' voices remained, more panicked and louder than before.

I could pick out my own, could hear my mate falling only a few wingspans away, and my son cry out desperately for help.

Terror lend me new, seemingly inexhaustible strength. Pushed forward by the need to protect, I beat my wings hard, circling around two trees.

A vessel clung to the bark of the one behind that. Raiders with flight suits wrestled nets filled with the downy forms of our young into it, while others battled the last handful of survivors.

One of the aliens shouted something as it gestured expansively. The strange sounds leaving its mouth made no sense to me, and the waving motion of its arms only stoked my anger.

Did this creature think we would just let them have our young and leave? What kind of barbarous society had spawned these things, where a life was worth so little? Where another's youngling was nothing but prey, caught and sold for the sweet sound of their begging?

With a cry of outrage, I dove for the alien, letting the spear fly.

They didn't expect me, didn't look my way, and the weapon buried itself deep into the offending alien's torso.

It staggered back, surprised but alive.

That it was hit seemed to agitate the others because they shouted and pointed immediately, and a whole barrage of light flashed in retaliation.

Provided a precious opening, the remaining villagers dove in to strike at the aliens.

Burning pain blossomed all over my body, even though I whirled and evaded.

I tried to get to the fledglings, but they were too far away, the miserable creatures still too numerous. Quickly, my fellow warriors fell like leaves around me. I knew then that I would die, that there was nothing I could do but take as many of those carrion worms with me as the last heartbeats of this life afforded me.

So I dove forward with utter abandon and somehow broke through, grabbing one of the raiders with my feet and riding it to the ground. It struggled and cried until my claws ripped its neck apart with vicious rage and painted the hull of its metallic ship a dark blue. One of them I hit with my third wing, and it staggered, lost its footing, and fell.

Everyone trained their weapons on me. Another creature grabbed for something at its belt, waved it at me, and threw it.

I turned away in instinctual evasion.

Pain exploded at my back as I was pushed off the ship by an unseen force. The sudden loss of weight on the right side of my body left me unable to navigate. I couldn't hear anything anymore. My head was all confused, and my eyes seemed suddenly unable to focus correctly.

I flapped my wings, but all it did was turn me into a spin. Stunned, I watched as my falling form overtook the ripped-off remains of my right-side wings as they floated downward at a much more sedate pace.

No…

I…

NO!

One fretful look upward verified that the last of my comrades had been slain. The creatures scrambled into their ship. Thrusters lit up at the back of it.

My boy… my handsome boy, with his voice as clear as morning dew…

All the other children…

I had failed.

I would die.

No one would come for them.

My back hit a thick bushel of leaves, and the pain jerked me out of my miserable acceptance of death.

No! No way would I just die here!

With claws and hands, I groped for the leaves, ripping them in my desperate bid to find purchase. Finally, I managed to hold on to one, but my weight pulled it down inexorably. My hands, slick with blood, wouldn't be able to stay on it for long.

In a last-ditch effort, I slashed at the stem with my upper left wing, cutting through the thick fibers, then hooking into it.

Again I fell, but the leaf filled with the updraft and slowed my descent.

The pain threatened to rip me in half, and I blacked out several times until I saw the shadowy ground rise to meet me, too quickly for comfort.

Shit, I would not survive this.

And even if, what then?

My whole village was gone.

The nearest settlement was two days away.

And even if someone happened by, my people didn't fly down into the shadows.

It was considered the worst of luck to fall this low, to fall into the pit of mythological predators none had seen in generations.

Who would ever find me there?

# CHAPTER THREE

## THE GUARDIAN

THE DARKNESS RECEDED SLOWLY, AND WITH IT, THE ringing in my ears and the pounding in my head.

And those horrible, horrible nightmares.

Around me, everything was silent. The sounds typically pervading the forest at all hours of day and night had been replaced by a very low, almost inaudible hum. The foul smells of decay and earth I would expect at the foot of the trees were notably absent, as was the fresh, moist air of the upper branches. Instead, the air was dry and cool, feeling almost... unnatural.

"Ah, you are awake," a voice I'd never heard before stated. It was strangely unfeeling and crisp, almost neutral in tone, while perfectly enunciated. The way it echoed harshly led me to believe we were in a small, enclosed space.

When I blinked open my eyes to take a look at my surroundings, my estimation proved right. Metal and glass surfaces locked me in from all sides. Everything seemed orderly and clean, very alien and jarring.

I was laid out on my stomach, on some kind of table or such. A haslaroid form moved to stand in my field of vision. My first instinct was to panic, then confusion overcame me, as it again opened its mouth to produce my language, which it shouldn't be capable of, given its anatomy. Then the shiny metal exterior of the creature hit home, and I understood what I was seeing.

By the Mother! This had to be a dream! I died, and this was some strange illusion meant to shorten the time between one life and the next. It had to be!

The creature looked at me with what seemed expectant curiosity.

I realized belatedly that my thoughts had drowned out its words.

"I'm sorry," I croaked, "What did you say?"

"I said," it chirped, "You were gravely wounded, but you will pull through. How do you feel?"

"Thirsty," was the first thing that sprang to mind, and I couldn't seem to stop my beak from formulating the thought.

"Understandable," my mythical benefactor agreed, "You drink rainwater caught in the leaves and crevices of the trees as well as fruit juices, yes?"

I nodded slowly.

"Very well, I will get you some," it decided, "Please do not move while I'm gone. It might aggravate your wounds or even reopen them."

I nodded again, dazed.

The alien turned to leave through the door materializing from nothingness in one of the sterile metallic walls, the surface of which looked eerily like the creature's skin.

A set of enormous wings extended out the broad back

before its feet completely hit the forest floor, and it shot upward, out of sight. The door closed again.

A guardian.

I'd just met one of the all-knowing wanderers. It had found and saved me.

What were the odds?

# CHAPTER FOUR

## DESPERATE ANGER

"I'm sorry, *First Female to fly in the open Sky*," the guardian shook his head as he walked through the door separating cockpit from what seemed like the primary storage and living space, where he'd laid me out on a cushy mattress on the ground, "I consulted the Great Neutrality's databases and asked all space station and ships within ten lightyears in all directions for permission to comb through their sensor data. 352 stations and 5,491 ships allowed my request. Still, I could find no trace of the ship you described. None of them hold a record of having seen them."

"No! That's impossible! Someone must have!" agitated motions flickered through my wings. I wanted to stand and walk around, but the guardian deemed acting on such impulses 'counterproductive to the healing process' and forbade it, "Someone must have seen them!"

"I concur," the metallic figure knelt by my side.

He'd introduced himself as Allarand, and when I told him my name, a strange expression crossed his face. Strange, like everything else around here. Like everything else about him. "Still, I can't find them. I also searched all databases available to me for Karrkuishian younglings being offered for sale, but there have been no notifications as of yet."

"Well, it's only been two days...," I intertwined my claws nervously, "And you said they will most likely want to make sure the chicks are healthy, first, ...to assess their worth, right?"

Allarand shook his head, gently lifting the bandage to check on my wound, it felt like. At least, I thought so... the haslaroid shape was so different from what I knew ...from what I was comfortable with...

His voice was cool and detached as he prodded my back, "*First Female to fly in the open Sky*, I will keep on looking, but I'm afraid it is pointless. From what little intelligence I could gather, I compute that this was a private venture. Most likely, your younglings were kidnapped for a specific purpose."

"Like some rich asshole's zoo, you mean?" I snapped, only to regret it instantly.

One didn't snap at a guardian. And he had saved my life. By the old rites, I owed him a great big debt for this alone. BUT, DAMN, WAS I ANGRY!

Was this a cruel joke of Sister Fate?

Against all odds, I'd not only survived the attack, the grenade, and the fall but also been found by a FUCKING GUARDIAN! Someone with greater reach than most planets' governors and royal houses! I'd been given the great honor and opportunity to ask a question, and he couldn't find the answer? How was that even possible??

The metallic figure leaned back to look me in the eyes, cocking his head slightly.

Shivers ran up and down my spine as I fully realized my misstep. Fear and panic spread in the wake of my horrendous disrespect for everything he was, everything he stood for. Some deeply ingrained instinct reasserted itself. Knowledge and behavior every fledgling was taught through story and myth long before they took to the air for the first time.

"I'm so sorry, All-knowing One, I didn't mean...," I struggled to rise and turn, just so I could bow down before him—a gesture that was hard to pull off while lying flat on one's stomach, "Please! I didn't mean to offend! I—"

"I understand," he put one hand on my unscathed shoulder and pushed me back down.

This simple gesture held in itself the strength of a dozen men, confined by the measured calculation born from an eternity of practice.

"Undoubtedly, this is very hard for you," he acknowledged, "I understand, and I am sorry that this plight has befallen you."

For some reason, this simple, almost neutral utterance made me choke up. Tears sprang into my eyes unbidden, and my feathering started to shiver uncontrollably.

"Please, Honorable Guardian!" I pleaded, "There must be something left to do! Some way to find them! They're all that's left of my village! They're helpless chicks, ripped from their home for Mother-knows what evil purpose! If you can't find them, who could? Please! I beg you!"

With a sigh, Allarand shook his head, "You asked me a question, and I have to answer if I can. I will continue searching for as long as you take to heal. No longer."

"Thank you, Honorable Guardian!" I made the sign of respect and thanks, "Father be praised!"

Only once he was gone again, and the healing mixture he'd provided dragged me down into a sleep full of disjointed, horrible nightmares born from memory, did I realize my folly. Even if I knew where they were... how would I ever get the little ones back?

Me, one lonely, broken warrior with only two wings, bloody and desperate, without resources or transportation?

Me, all alone in the universe.

# CHAPTER FIVE

## WINGS

"I recommend you have them removed," the all-knowing one propounded, "I could perform the operation if you wish."

I barely felt the prodding of his fingers through the haze of painkillers. Or maybe it was the grief jealously holding me wrapped inside a tight bind. Half a month had passed, and everything seemed like a strange dream by now. A dream that might end once I left this shuttle, left this strange world of which Allarand was the gatekeeper.

Like Keeper of the Roots, the nebulous mythical being standing watch over the gate to the underworld. Maybe that one would be the next person guiding me along on my journey. Maybe I would meet him once I left this place.

I probably deserved to.

After all, I'd aggravated my wounds more than once to lengthen the healing process. I'd done it in small, cautious increments, hoping my healer wouldn't notice.

*Allarand would tell me later that he had but thought it an understandable reaction to his ultimatum and that he, therefore, was the one to blame for giving me the wrong incentive.*

*He wasn't, though. My conduct was despicable, contemptible, and highly disrespectful. I knew it even with the limited intellectual facilities the constant drip of medicine, memories, and survivor's guilt permitted me.*

I blinked, confused by his words, "Remove? Remove whom?"

Was he finally fed up with me taking up his time? Was he finally pushing me out the door?

"Your remaining wings," he clarified, "Your body is strong enough now to endure the strain of the operation. Your chances of dying are below 0.02 % if I were to perform it."

"WHAT? You want to cut off my wings? The two I still have?" I couldn't believe Allarand was even considering this, "NO! NO WAY! I already lost half of them!"

I wasn't quite sure why I clung to life, why I clung to my broken body. Why I stretched out the inevitable. What was the purpose of it all? Allarand still hadn't found the chicks, and he wasn't even giving me daily updates anymore. It didn't take a genius to understand the implications. They were gone. I would never find them.

If a guardian couldn't, what chance did I have?

No, this was the end of the branch. I was the last of my village.

And no other village would take me with my wings missing. Whether two or four, it didn't matter... Unable to provide for myself, unable to fight and hunt, which was all I'd ever been proficient at, I was useless. No community wanted to feed a useless stranger.

I was reminded of a pauper I'd seen in the large settlement. A veteran of another species' war, my father explained. He'd been missing half his upper right wing. A detriment, to be sure, but he would still have been able to fly. Still, cast out, there had been no place for him anywhere else but at the lowest levels of that wretched place, begging for the essentials needed to prolong an existence deemed unworthy by the old ways.

Only missing half of one wing.

Now look at me.

By the Mother! What a perfectly wretched thing I was to impose on a guardian of all people, keep him engaged in my healing, and keep him rooted to this shadowy realm!

In moments like these, I asked myself why he even bothered. He treated me like he had all the time in the universe, like it didn't matter at all if he stayed in this ugly, lightless underbelly of the woods for a month, a year, or a decade.

Wasn't he supposed to wander around? Wasn't he feeling a need to do so? A growing itching sensation, much like I did for the lack of flying, for open spaces? Wasn't he supposed to provide all these people with the opportunity to ask questions? Why did the one person holding all the answers seem as aimless as I felt?

"FIRST FEMALE TO FLY IN THE OPEN SKY," he sighed and sat down next to me, "I understand that your kind is proud of their ability to fly. And rightly so. It is a rare gift of nature. Your whole society and way of life revolve around it. Not being able to fly will not just make it hard for you to get around; it will exclude you largely from your society's daily life."

I swallowed and nodded. Society. Others like me. How was I ever to face others of my kind, being the last survivor, being broken like this?

A tear sprang into my eye, unbidden. I already knew

what he was going to say next. The missing weight on the right side of my back made it all too apparent.

Pain flared up there. Remembered pain. The panicked frenzy of falling, strangely dull and removed from the present moment.

"However," he continued, "Unless you can afford and find someone who can provide you with a new set of right-side wings, you will not fly again in any case. Carrying around your left-side wings will unbalance you. They will atrophy, hinder your progress, and, over time, adjusting for their weight will distort your posture, bring pain to your body and weaken your frame. Removing them as well is your best option for survival."

As my mind struggled to rise above the numbness of physical and emotional trauma, fighting it out on the battle-ground of my soul, I contemplated the truth in his words. Everything he said was bound to be true. Guardians couldn't lie; everyone knew this.

It was still hard to accept his truth, to accept what was best.

And why should I?

"And who would care?" I croaked, "Who would know? As you pointed out, I have no place here anymore. All I can do is sit at the roots and wait for the Keeper to open the ground for me. I don't need to fly to go into the deep. I will manage the short way without proper balance. If you just open the shuttle door, I can..."

Allarand stared at me, his face emotionless and still. Whatever I'd planned to say, dribbled away into noth-ingness.

After several heartbeats, he asked, "This Keeper, he sounds like an interesting character. Please, tell me about him."

He would do that all the time, ask me about myths and stories of my people, the village, and my family. Knowing I'd never refuse him. Knowing I'd been taught to respond to his kind with the utmost respect and courtesy, to fulfill a guardian's request without doubt or hesitation.

This wasn't even factoring in the enormous debt my honor urged me to pay off, when my mind still didn't know how to go about it.

And, to be completely honest, I welcomed the change in subject matter. My cowardly heart was still too enamored with the concept of life to follow the bragging of my voice down the sensible and honorable path.

In this strange place, the loss of my world and myself seemed so far removed at times, only to fill out every nook and cranny whenever I closed my eyes.

We didn't talk about it again for two days.

Then Allarand made me stand up and walk, and I felt it. It was horrible.

"Let's go for a walk outside," he ordered, holding out one metallic arm for me to cling to.

I was so focused on the strange, exhausting motions that I hardly noticed where we were headed. Only once he stopped did I look up.

Rows and rows of small mounts of earth, topped with stones, leaves, and braided roots, stretched out to all sides around me. Weapons, amulets, and other personal items were carefully placed inside the burial ornaments.

I swallowed. Something hard and unyielding lodged itself in my throat in light of the overwhelming display of care and respect.

"You buried them," a tear ran down my cheek, "You buried all of them."

"There was no one else. You were in no condition to do so," Allarand explained, "And, according to your people's traditions, it would have been disrespectful to leave them for the animals to feed on, correct?"

"Yeah," I nodded, dazed. To bury all of them, to prepare all these offerings..., "This must have taken days!"

"11 of your days, 42 hours, and 5.38 minutes," he confirmed.

"But... don't you, ahem, don't you have better things to do?" I shook my head, "I mean, I'm thankful! Thank you so much for doing all of this! I could have never... but... Allarand, why are you still here? Why do you bother yourself with me and mine?"

The metallic figure smiled at me.

He smiled!

Then he said, "Do you know whom a guardian asks if they have a question?"

I blinked. Every chick knew that, "They ask those that ask them."

"No," he shook his bald head, "I mean a question that cannot be answered by a mortal."

"They... could ask another guardian, maybe? Or maybe the Great Neutrality as a whole?"

"Well...," he turned to the left and started walking again, gently tugging me along, "There are questions even the Great Neutrality can not answer. After all, if we could answer all questions, why would we bother asking any?"

I nodded, once more very self-conscious of my wobbly gait.

"I have a question like that, and I asked it," he made a grand gesture, "to the universe, to reality itself.

Chance brought me here, made me aware of your plight. So now, I have to decide if you are the answer, the path to it, or if our meeting was just a freak accident. But, regardless of what I don't know, regardless of what I would like to examine further, I also feel the pull inside that tells me to move on."

When he stopped again, it was in front of an open grave. A flat, large bundle lay inside, neatly wrapped and fastidiously decorated with flowers, feathers, and braided branches. With my feathers... Those were my wings. This was my grave.

"I couldn't find your chicks," the all-knowing one confessed, "So I still owe you an answer. I will give you another three days to come up with a different question. Because I'm curious what it might be and what it might set in motion. But that's all the time I can give you. Furthermore, I will close this last grave when night darkens the leaves this evening. So, if you want anything else in there, you have another 26 hours, 3.1 minutes to deposit it."

I swallowed hard.

Standing here, in front of my own grave, made me painfully aware of the wind whispering in my feathers, of the light playing all around, and the smell of the air, the song of life unfolding, worming its way into my skull, into my heart.

Mother, I didn't want to die!

Maybe lying down in that hole was the sensible thing to do, the honorable thing. But it wasn't my thing. I didn't want this!

And my wings... Hanging on to this part of my body would only harm it in the future, would harm me... The all-knowing one was here now, offering medical help of a quality I would never be able to afford—even if I could find someone selling it. And I wouldn't even know where to start looking for someone like that ...not around here, that was for sure, not in the next village—if that still existed, that was—not anywhere on this planet, perhaps.

And he was offering it for free.

But... where would I go without wings? Where *could* I go?

# CHAPTER SIX

## QUESTIONS AND DECISIONS

I**T TOOK TWO DAYS FOR MY BODY TO SLEEP OFF THE** anesthesia and for my mind to be somewhat clear and coherent once more.

When Allarand finally helped me up and outside, my mind recognized the rightness of my decision in the suddenly less lopsided gait and my heart the wrongness of it in the missing weight on my back. It seemed even stranger to walk now... my whole balance was off, and I stumbled frequently, then tried to steady myself using two sets of limbs, whose absence my body hadn't yet internalized, which only made it worse. If not for my benefactor's timely interventions, my face would have left a few nice dents in the earthy forest floor.

Great Mother, I bumbled about like a chick fresh from the egg... though I was pretty certain I didn't look half as cute in doing so.

Thankfully, Allarand was tactful enough not to comment or show any signs of pity or amusement as he guided me back to the burial site.

"I decided to wait for your recovery before I closed the grave," he informed me.

I stopped dead in my tracks, and he froze in his movements so as not to pull me off-balance.

"But you said you would close it come nightfall," I was sure I remembered correctly, "So if you didn't, that renders your previous statement a lie."

"Yes, I did. And no, it doesn't," there was the slightest brightening of his orange eye-lights, "At the time I made that statement, this is what I was convinced would happen. But when you decided to accept the operation, that occupied me for several hours. Afterward, I felt it would be unwise of me not to monitor you until you woke and ensure everything had proceeded smoothly. Nighttime had long since come and gone when all was said and done, rendering my previous announcement irrelevant."

"So... you thought I wouldn't take the operation," chills ran down my spine.

"In fact, I calculated very favorable odds that you would," the smallest of smiles crossed his lips. It was so fleeting I wasn't sure if it had actually been there or just a figment of my imagination.

"Did you... Do you mean to say you tricked yourself?"

"That information is outside the normal realm of conversation," he informed me, "Is this the new question you want answered?"

"No," I shook my head, "But I thought about it. I have a new question. Maybe I can ask it after... you know."

He nodded, "That sounds like a good time for it."

We entered the little grove he'd turned into my village's final resting place and made our way to my grave. A second bundle lay atop the first now, wrapped tight and furnished with handmade gifts meant to ease the way down the roots. My wings had no soul. They didn't need all that scuttling.

*At the time, I didn't understand Allarand's intention and foresight. At the time, I just thought it a nice gesture.*

*But even then, Allarand knew me. Because he'd know uncounted individuals just like me, and people are not as unique as we like to pretend we are.*

*The immortal wanderer had calculated what I would most likely ask and what it would allow him to do long before my mind had formulated the question.*

"Allarand, what will I have to do for you to take me with you, to show me the wonders of the universe, to tell me the greatest secret you know?" my eyes were still locked onto the pockmarked earth in front of me.

He'd created such a beautiful, peaceful place, yet its implications made me despair. Having sanctified this ground, his part here was done. He would leave me with nothing but the ghosts of the dead and two feet to walk on. Fear made me shiver inside.

"That is a lot to ask," he kept his eyes ahead a moment longer, "But if you swear your life to me, I would be glad to take you on," he turned to look at me, "I do enjoy your company, Songbird."

"'Songbird'?" turning his way, I cocked my head.

Allarand almost smiled, "Your name gets very long in translation, FIRST FEMALE TO FLY IN THE OPEN SKY, and when we go to other places, I need something to call you. There might not always be time for proper decorum."

"I see," I took a deep breath, "So I would be your servant, then?"

Not that I had a problem with that. It would be an honorable way to repay the life debt I owed, never mind what other benefits it could gain me. The lure of his unfathomably extensive knowledge, of being able to understand and make sense of things I hadn't even heard of yet, was a potent one even to someone in my muddled state of mind. But for the most part, I was just desperate not to be left behind.

*Even if he'd told me straight-up he was going to kill me in the end, I would probably have agreed to his terms. Maybe I'd always had more in common with my mythical namesake than I realized...*

And even though I had no inclination to go to the stars, the hope that weightlessness might make me forget I couldn't actually fly anymore, might dull the painful itch inside, was a potent persuasion all in itself.

*Oh, what a naive little birdy I'd been back then.*

"More like a travel companion," Allarand gestured vaguely, "I do not need anyone to perform menial work for me. Consider this, though: I will have the last word on things. On some of your decisions. I will be bound to protect the knowledge you seek. Once you learn it, I cannot allow you to leave. Once you learn it, I will ask the question that will equipoise yours."

"I see."

*No, I really didn't.*

*I knew even back then that I should have weighed my options longer and thought up different avenues my life might take.*

*But desperation makes pliant fools out of all of us, and I didn't.*

I just swallowed and nodded.

"So, you will come with me," he ventured a calculated guess.

"Yes," I nodded again.

Regardless of the pressure inside or outside, it was of my own free will that I bowed deeply, then knelt in front of him. I had to momentarily brace myself against the ground with my outstretched hands, or I would have toppled over. But once I found my equilibrium again, I crossed my arms over my chest, touching the opposite shoulders with my outstretched fingers, and declared, "Master."

# CHAPTER SEVEN

## A HORRIBLE IDEA

*Neutral Space, circa 8 Human standard years prior*

"Please, Master Allarand!" I shook my head despairingly, "I don't understand why you would even consider going there."

The all-knowing one looked at me. I could swear, he was making some kind of face, even though—as he liked to explain to me repeatedly—his people got the principle and all, but they did not make faces. Period.

Still, more than one standard rotation had been ample time to get accustomed to the obvious as well as the subtle expressions which had been so alien to me at the beginning.

He had also introduced me to many other races at this point, every last one as different in anatomy, beliefs, and expression to my kind as he was.

"I do not follow," his orange eyes blinked.

"Yours is the most knowledgeable and wise species in the known universe. How can you actually consider going to this... magical ritual thingy? And to a Haslar planet, no less! In the middle of Mother-forsaken Central Haslar Command Space!" I threw up my arms.

There was a smirk; I was so damned sure there was. No faces, my tail feathers!

Other than that smirk, the robot didn't move a nanite.

As a wanderer, he was designed to be instantly recognizable, his body built as a checksum of most haslaroid life-forms and completely glazed in a silvery metallic sheen, his eyes orange rings of light on a black backdrop, his head bald. By now, I knew it was all for show. Like the entirety of the Great Neutrality was made up of units, he was made up of more submicroscopic parts than there were inhabitants in a barkborer colony.

"And what about that new body?" I argued.

"What new body?"

"The one you've been tinkering with in the cargo bay," I made a vague motion to the back of the cockpit, "I figured you're just about done with it since there's only the face missing. Don't you have to be extra careful with protecting your super-advanced technology?"

He nodded, "You are right, of course. And it is very well protected, no matter my presence."

*Okay, begging then...*

"Master Allaraaaaaand," I did that chirpy sound in the back of my throat he found so 'exceedingly interesting,' "I implore you. Is this really where we need to go? The Haslars are slavemongers on a grand scale, and they scare me."

"You fear they would violate the neutrality of my species?"

I fell back into my seat. I knew where this—and we— were heading, "No, no one would ever mess with your people; every child knows better."

"Then you are concerned I will not protect you adequately? "

I'd seen his moves. No, that wasn't the point.

My shoulders scrunched up slightly as the empty joint sockets in my back hurt with that echo of pain I could never fully forget. The naked skin atop wouldn't grow any new feathers. After realizing the suddenly very real danger of sunburn and how naked and vulnerable the empty patch made me feel, Allarand had tailored three beautiful vests to my unusual proportions from a richly patterned, velvety cloth, which he'd seen me admire at a local bazaar on one of the many planets we'd visited.

I was wearing one of them now. The concept of donning clothes on a daily basis had been alien to me. Back home, we had some ceremonial garb, for special occasions only. To have your feathers flattened by some external layer hindered their optimal use, especially their performance in flight. Which was why we normally only wore the rings. I fingered the three dark circles on my upper arm nervously.

Besides, we weren't victims to the elements like many of the species I kept encountering. Well ...I was now, so I understood the need for clothing, was even getting accustomed to it. Like I was getting used to so many things I would have found wonderous or even ludicrous in the past.

Having fought uncounted rotations to become a free warrior of the third level, I was also still getting used to being a servant. Allarand wasn't making this one any easier on me when he let me roam free, be my own person most of the time, and even encouraged me to speak my mind, only to crack down on me unyieldingly whenever one of those rare occasions came around where he deemed it appropriate to make the decision for me.

"I know this is your call to make. You're the master;

I'm the servant," my fingers got preoccupied with a decorative button in the same color and design as the rings around my upper arm.

A subtle shift in his demeanor conveyed a strange sort of warmth as he reached out to take my hands in his.

My gaze dropped to the floor, "I... I just don't want to go there."

He knew why, damn it!

But then, who was I to dare question him at all?

"And what if there is something interesting to learn from all this?" Allarand's eyes moved in a way I recognized as plotting a course. They dimmed down for the barest fraction of a second, and I felt a strange distance in the glowing orange rings as he connected to the shuttle's computer.

"What do I need to know about Haslars? They are evil, selfish killers that enslave whole worlds!"

...that send slavers to ravish those planets and people they had no official claim over...

Like those that killed my village, that took my son...

Unbidden thoughts of home—what had been home—, bubbled up inside.

The old desperation rose with it, a bitter taste that choked me, then plunged a heavy, acid-dripping lance into my heart.

My back hurt some more.

"Have you ever met one?"

I jumped up, roaming the cockpit, trying to eliminate the prickling sensation running through my claws. Even though I'd shortened them and trained myself to tread softly so as to diminish the effect, they still clicked harshly on the bare metallic floor, filling the small space with the sound of barely restrained anger, "I don't need to. Besides, what's this Haslar high priestess to you, anyhow?"

The all-knowing one watched me, his eyes following my movements as I checked random numbers and letters on the screens. There was an unusual delay in his response time.

"High Priestess Governor Sh'Zal'Lagesh is an old acquaintance," he finally said.

This gave me pause. Was that amiable warmth in his voice?

"I have to go. She explicitly asked for this unit to be present as a witness at the annual ZH'tha'ga," he made a gesture, some uncommonly vague shooing motion, "And you swore to go where I go."

So I did.

I sat back down, my head bowed, my honor horrified by my bad behavior, "Of course, Master. I'm sorry for my rash and uncouth words. I didn't mean to insult your ...acquaintance."

There was this slight flicker in his eye lights.

*Thinking back to that moment, I would often wonder if it was the one that sealed my fate and locked me in my path. Would he have let me persuade him if I argued differently or with more finesse? And if so, would it have changed what happened or merely postponed the inevitable?*

Allarand nodded, then pointed at the small room his shuttle had cordoned off for my use, "Once we arrive, leave your rings. All of them."

I swallowed hard.

# CHAPTER EIGHT

## THE AIDE

*HALI'LLE'LESH, HASLAR CENTRAL COMMAND SPACE, CIRCA 8 HUMAN STANDARD YEARS PRIOR*

"Your aide?" the Haslar female looked me up and down like a piece of freshly hung meat. Mostly down. "I've never heard of an all-knowing one with an aide."

"Are you questioning the integrity of this unit?" Allarand asked.

He persisted in calling me his aide when introducing me to others, explaining once that the concept of servitude had a bad rep in most systems and that he didn't want to risk exposing me to any "disagreeable behaviors".

Several jewels rose in rapid fashion above the Haslar's eyes. Had there been a hairline, they would have vanished in it. These peoples' utter baldness made them utterly creepy in my eyes. My time with Allarand had accustomed me to being the only one present sporting feathers in most situations. Still, hair was, in principle, similar enough, and most haslaroids had at least some.

However, where other haslaroids tended to have eyebrows, Haslars embedded these gems in their skin. The more gems they sported, the tougher they were. The tougher they were, the more clout they had. The more magic they could wield.

Dominating warrior societies, had to love those...

Magic... what a fascinating concept. I'd seen some wondrous things since leaving home, and magic was undoubtedly the most intriguing. My people did possess some. I'd seen it firsthand when my parents took me to a demonstration in that large settlement, but all in all, it was very new to me.

In one of our conversations, Allarand had speculated that maybe we were too new a species and that magic would grow stronger and more widespread with us in time.

Haslars... now those bastards had been around forever, and if not for the restrictions put on them by the guardians, they would have probably taken over the whole universe by now. Not at least because of the magic and the magitech they possessed.

"NO! Of course not!" this one carried around five stones in her head, not very impressive, "I wouldn't dare, All-knowing One! It's just that... this is unheard of. No member of a slave race has ever been allowed to see the ZH'tha'ga!"

The guardian laid a warning hand on my shoulder. What seemed like a gesture of emphasis was holding me back without any noticeable effort. In times like these, machine strength was a bummer.

"This one is of a free people."

"But she is your aide."

"Yes. And that does not lessen her existential worth in any way."

Now the Haslar looked at me like I was some kind of deadly disease.

*Please, Master, let me give her a bloody nose!*, I thought.

Then I remembered that I had to activate that transmission thingy in my head first if I wanted him to hear. I thought the command, then repeated my plea, 'Please, Master, may I knock her brains out?'

'Compose yourself, Songbird. This one has no understanding of freedom as you do. She has been molded by her upbringing. For her, freedom is to know one's place.'

'And to not be a slave. Slavery is for other, lesser races.'

'Maybe you do not understand them as thoroughly as you believe. Besides, she wears a gem that enhances her strength and agility. Even with the advantage your greater size provides, an attack has meager chances of success.'

I did the mind-grumble.

Meanwhile, the normal discussion had concluded without me.

"Fine," the Haslar said, "I will get her a pass and warn the guards not to disturb her."

"You are very gracious," Allarand bowed.

She bowed in return.

I knew what was coming next. This never got old.

"Please, may I ask a question, All-knowing One?"

"You may ask; this unit will answer if it is allowed to."

The Haslar woman looked at me, a slight hesitation in her gaze.

I snatched a datapad from the pouch at my belt and stood at attention as if to write down every private word of her inquiry. She looked at him. He looked at me. I looked at him. He looked at her, then back at me. I rolled my eyes and turned around, taking long strides toward a nearby window.

Whatever! As if I was interested in what that slave-monger considered the most important question of her life...

That feedback sound in my head sounded suspiciously like a snort. I grinned.

Besides, my question had made Allarand take me with him. As far as I knew, no one else had ever managed that.

*Eat your heart out, Haslar Bitch!*


The window was big and pretentious, and there was nothing but darkness on the other side. It worked great with the rest of the place.

Hali'lle'lesh was one of the outer core planets of the second-most-important solar system in Haslar space. It wasn't actually livable. Even Haslars needed air, so they'd built a big city under a big dome made of some glittering crystalline stuff. Never having seen anything like it before, I could only guess at what it was made of.

This window was part of said dome, a quirky technical detail made possible by the fact that the small spaceport stood as gate to the city at the very rim of it. Outside there was only gray dust, darkness, and a handful of stars way above. When we descended toward the planet, the blue sun central to this system had reigned over it in silent majesty, but down here, its light was still some way off.

"There's nothing much to see this way, is there?" the Haslar boy crept out of the shadows like a ghost to stand beside me, following my gaze, "Mom says it's like life. If you don't have strength, it looks like this. Bleak, empty, and dead."

"There are the stars," I reminded him.

Since my beak couldn't produce the strange sounds most haslaroids called language, Allarand had outfitted me with a slim necklace containing a built-in speaker. It was connected to the tech he'd implanted in my brain, which incorporated, among other things, a translator, and the insertion of which was one of those rare decisions my master had decreed for me.

It had taken some time to get used to, but by then, all I needed to do was think the answer, and the necklace produced the spoken words, adjusting pitch, loudness, and tone of voice to match my intent.

"Yes, that's what I say. There's always hope if there are stars," he gazed up, a strange longing crossing his features, "I want to go there when I'm older. I want to see all the stars, all the known universe! Where are you from? You look funny."

"Funny? Have you never seen a 'slave race' before?"

"How would I? There are no other races allowed in the capital. Because of the temple and all," the boy scrunched up his face. "Besides, I heard the wanderer. You're not of a slave race!"

We shared a moment of comfortable silence while he looked me up and down.

Then he asked, "Can I touch you? Please?"

"WHAT?"

Yeah, I laid a bit more drama into that performance than was necessary. But he was just on the verge between not knowing and knowing too well, age-wise. And hell, he was a Haslar, after all. Maybe he did mean it like...

"No, I didn't mean like THAT!" his golden skin on his high cheekbones darkened into the most adorable copper shade I had ever seen.

"I mean, just... like... like just shake hands or something... Like, don't you people do that?"

"How would you know what 'we people' do?"

He turned even more coppery, "I read about it…"

"Your Mom lets you read about us people? Ain't that corruption of youngsters?"

"Corruption? Isn't that if you have bad genes?"

How could any Haslar be so cute? That was unfair!

Another moment of silence crept between us.

His perfect golden skin was unadorned, I noticed. Allarand had told me that this ceremony we were about to attend was about some Haslar kids getting their first stones, but compared to the others of his kind I'd seen since my arrival, the boy's outward appearance did seem a bit strange.

"Say, don't you… like… aren't you supposed to have wings?" he finally sputtered, "I mean, you have feathers, so…"

"Well," I cocked my head as I looked down at his tiny form, "Aren't you supposed to have gems all over your body? I mean, you're a Haslar, right?"

He turned coppery again and looked away quickly.

It took him another few heartbeats to recover, but with the persistence seemingly universal in youngsters, he said, "Hey, would you like a better view? I know the best window around! Follow me!"

And off he went, his slightly too long arms and legs trying to keep up with the purpose in his stride.

Absolutely adorable… My son might have been his age now.

Might have been.

I shook my head and looked back at Allarand and the Haslar woman. The guardian held her hand, observing something on her skin… or in it. He might be doing a genetic test on her. I saw him do that once. It would only take a moment.

A small crowd of people already gathered at a short distance from the two, however, waiting respectfully to be noticed and allowed to ask their questions.

So my master was busy for the time being...

Besides, if I got in trouble, I could always brain-shout for help.

Copper-boy lead me to the other side of the small complex, up a flight of stairs, and into a kind of observatory dome. I could see the city from there, all of it.

Built like honeycombs, the houses were getting taller and more opulent toward the middle. It seemed that the tallest building in the dead center of town had an observatory as well. The entire top floor connected with the protective crystalline structure. They were one. In the distance, sunlight moved in, creating a sharp divide between light and darkness.

"Is that...?" I asked.

"The temple, yeah. Ain't it pretty?"

Not just pretty, I had to admit to myself, it was absolutely gorgeous! The wavy lines and big glass windows were not what I'd expected from the Haslars. Yes, technologically, they were highly advanced, but they were a savage people, bringing war, destruction, and slavery to half the known universe. How could they build something so... perfect?

"It's nice," I allowed, "Who built it?"

"They say the ancient elders had it built. The machines still work to their specifications."

"What machines?"

"Like... everything, I guess. Except for the newer ships and stuff," he shrugged, "I don't know about the temple;

I wasn't inside yet. I wasn't allowed until now. But they say there are some great big machines there."

"Like what?"

"Like the sun lens!"

"What's that?"

He opened his mouth, then shut it.

"I'm not allowed to say."

"You mean, you don't know?" I stifled a smirk, since the alien expression might have frightened the boy. It once made some other aliens think it was a precursor of me trying to eat them. Only Allarand's quick intervention had stopped them from riling up their whole village for a bird hunt. One might think I should have learned my lesson not to wander off in strange environments on that occasion alone. ...*Well, what can I say?*

The kid held the air of an expert around him like a cloak for a moment longer, then his shoulders sank down a fraction. I noticed a small hump next to his shoulder bone. It looked quite peculiar, "What is—"

# CHAPTER NINE

## THE CROW

"Hey, looky there! Seems like the scum-kid found himself some slave-scum to hang with!"

My companion jerked. Children's laughter followed the acid remark. Suddenly there was a whole horde of golden little pricks encroaching on us. I took two steps back until I felt the window shield me from behind.

There were six of them, two boys and four girls. A big girl with broad shoulders and beady black eyes was leading them. Her clothes looked expensive; the upward bearing of her nose was too steep for my comfort. She didn't have a stone either. None of them did.

Fending them off shouldn't be too difficult... but I didn't want the trouble. Their parents had to be around, right?

Copper-boy mustered up and stepped in front of me. I could see in his gait that he would have preferred to run. His lean muscles and long legs might very well have been the result of running a lot and hiding in hard-to-reach spaces.

"She's not a slave, H'sa! She's a guardian's aide!

You better watch your words, or he might take offense and have you punished! "

The girl laughed, "Right! You and your vivid imagination, R'sal!"

Following her lead, the others also laughed. I noticed a small girl in the back, slim as a whip, all carefully administered tension. Whip-girl wasn't so much as smirking. Her eyes weren't on us like those of the others. Rather, she observed the whole room. I decided to absolutely not turn my back on that one.

Rich bully H'sa stopped the hilarity with a sharp motion of her arm, "Besides, what could this guardian punish me with? He has no rights on a Haslar world!"

"Right, like you don't know about Exagon 3-14," R'sal crossed his arms and leaned back.

"Exagon 3-14? What about it? It blew up in some freak mining accident."

"Yeah, right. That's what it was, sure," the boy's acting wasn't half bad. Whip-girl didn't seem to believe him, but H'sa swallowed it whole.

Her eyes narrowed, "What do you know? Spill it!"

"Just that there was no accident. My mom said some fool tried to snatch a guardian. He even managed to cut it off from the Great Neutrality for a while, wanted to study it, take it apart. But the robot freed itself, and when it reconnected, the Great Neutrality decided that something like that couldn't happen again and to make an example. The guardian took over the mining town and set the power core to explode! There was nothing anyone could do; it was unstoppable!"

I nodded severely, "Yeah, heard about that. I have no trouble believing it either. I've seen guardians work, you know. As the *aide* of one! I've seen things you wouldn't believe!"

Not that all-knowing ones had to resort to such barbarous behavior...

They were revered wherever they went, and that these little brats didn't appreciate the severity of their disrespect boggled my mind. But then, they were Haslars..., and Allarand had warned me beforehand that their kids were given a lot of freedom before being implanted their first stone in this ritual thingy.

H'sa and the boys turned wide eyes on me. They actually looked at me this time. Like I was there and worth noticing.

Whip-girl crossed her arms, "What about the guardian? Are we supposed to believe he just blew himself up?"

R'sal swallowed, his eyes racing back and forth.

"And why not?" I heard myself say, "Their limited number may be greatly revered by other species, but they are only gears in the machine. The sanctity of the Great Neutrality will always overrule the needs of the individual unit."

H'sa nodded, "He was compromised, so he was weak. His weakness could not be allowed to taint his race."

"I don't think he died," R'sal muttered, "Units get constantly uploaded to the Great Neutrality, don't they? So, wouldn't his consciousness live on there? Couldn't it be downloaded into another body?"

He looked at me with a strange light in his eyes.

It was very similar to when he'd told me about flying to the stars.

My thoughts momentarily drifting to that artificial body in our cargo bay, I shrugged, "Probably..."

"What nonsense are you telling these kids, You Wingless Bird?" the Haslar was on us like a freight shuttle in rush cycle. She grabbed whip-girl, shoved her into the arms of one of the two big fellows who followed in her wake, and just kept on going. The other kids jumped aside and bowed their heads.

Even R'sal took a step to the side. He started to speak, "She's a—"

"I don't care if she's your pet or your mother's!" the woman stopped right in front of me and narrowed her eyes, "This is a disgrace! Even H'Gar'esh should not be so brash and disrespectful as to bring ... *this* here," her gaze wandered off to look at the boy for a second, "Even if she has nothing to lose."

'Allarand, help! There's some crazy Haslar woman here; she might try to kill me! ...ALLARAND!!!' I thought.

The first of the Haslar men handled whip-girl like a Menurian vase: very breakable and very, very expensive, as he set her down gently and straightened out her festive gown, while the other stepped up behind their mistress, puffing up his sizable frame. I could still look down on both of them, but the number of glittering stones in all their heads left me unsure of the exact amount of danger I was in.

R'sal, meanwhile, fidgeted almost imperceptibly. Maybe his trepidation was warring with his wish to help me. Maybe what the woman just said had hurt him more than he let on. He didn't even look at me, though. There was a moment of stillness in his features as his gaze zoomed out into the distance. Then he bolted, weaving through the two bigger boys like a barkrunner, hitting the ground with his knees and sliding between the first Mr. Muscle's legs like a pro. Behind the small group, he jumped up with one fluid motion and sprinted away, his arms and robes flying.

The woman shook her head in disgust.

"Coward," she sneered, "You see, Children? That's what corrupt genes will do to you."

There was a low rumble of obedient agreement. Whip-girl crossed her arms, dark clouds roaming behind her black eyes.

Well, he was a Haslar and a kid, so I wasn't terribly shocked by his sudden flight.

I just wished I knew what amount or kind of magic I'd been left to face here.

The crazy lady wore a lot of jewelry, but not much of it on her face. With only seven stones on her forehead, her rank couldn't be that impressive, right?

I smiled sweetly, continuing our conversation as if nothing had happened between her derisive comment and my reply, "Whatever do you mean, Madam? I'm a very respectable sort. I was a top student in 'Intergalactic Diplomacy 101'!"

Her eyes grew wide like new wings had just spurted from my back or something, before constricting into tiny pinpricks, "You dare to address me, Slave Scum?"

Well, her punch certainly was impressive. I didn't even see it coming. Light exploded in my face as a crack echoed through my skull, starting somewhere in my lower beak. I was thrown back, and my head collided with the crystal. Pain flashed down my spine. Warm liquid poured down my face.

So the magic enhanced her physically. ... Great.

How had she even reached so high?

My hands found something to hold on to, and I tried to get back on my feet, blinking stupidly to scare away the stars in my vision.

The woman advanced on me. I gripped the railing tighter and focused my energy. Pushing myself off the window to get some leverage, I aimed for her knee, introducing a feint with my other foot. As suspected, she dodged the feint, and her unnatural speed made her vulnerable to my actual attack. There was a crunching sound as my foot hit her knee squarely, my claws slashing it open simultaneously. ...Well, they would have if I hadn't filed them down to bloody stumps so as not to aggravate my master whenever I walked around in his shuttle!

Still, she stumbled. Her momentum disturbed, she rushed past me and almost collided with the window too, screaming like an angry leaf beetle all the way.

There were gasps from the kids.

I clapped my beak.

*Take that, Haslar Bitch!*

Suddenly, the air itself grabbed me and pulled me up until my feet dangled over the floor by about half a meter. I felt like a rag doll as one of the musclemen frowned at me with silent disapproval, the fingers of one hand moving in that ritualistic way I'd come to associate with magic while he pressed his other index finger against a large turquoise gem over his right eye.

The woman got up, her leg slightly bent, her eyes spraying hateful sparks.

"You...," she hissed, "I will have you executed for this! I will have your feathers ripped out one by one until you bleed out, Slave Scum!"

"I'M NOT A DAMN SLAVE!" I roared.

Damn Haslars. Damn Allarand for bringing me here. What the hell had just happened? How had this gone sideways so damn fast?

The woman raised her fist, and fire bloomed into life around it.

"What is the meaning of this?" another female voice cut in.

Instant silence followed. The man holding me spun around and bowed deeply.

The magic holding me suspended cut out instantly, and my ass hit the ground. I asked my legs to do something about the drop as soon as I felt it, but they were utterly useless. Since everything else seemed to hurt, it didn't make much difference, anyway.

At least my eyes stopped tearing, so I could observe the procession of newcomers. A regal woman marched in front, her very expensive-looking robes complimented by an enormous headdress. I blinked in surprise as I realized that the big amber blotch on her forehead was a huge gem embedded right between her eyes. Cut to multifaceted perfection, it seemed to glow from the inside. Seven stones of different colors spread out on either side of it, forming two perfect arches. Four very muscled men with glittering brows trailed behind her.

Off to the side stood another woman, just as regal, with five stones over every brow. R'sal almost melted into that one's leg.

I thought there might be a slight resemblance between the two women and the boy, but my head hurt, and really, all Haslars looked so much alike with their unnatural golden skin and these emotionless black eyes.

Allarand slid up from behind like he was enjoying a quaint Sunday stroll. He stopped next to the boss lady and bowed to her.

She bowed back.

"Allarand, dear friend," she said, "Is this woman your aide? The one you told me about?"

He nodded, "Yes, this is her."

The woman who'd hit me blanched visibly. The kids stared at the woman and Allarand with unbridled wonder and admiration.

"I'm so sorry to find this situation has unfolded in my city. This is most disturbing," she half-turned back to one of the men, "Su'Lor here is a healer. He will have a look at her... "

"I appreciate your concern, High Priestess. However, this is not necessary."

'Not necessary?' I thought to him, 'Master, have you seen my face? I would think it's the least they could do!'

He gave me a disapproving look and stepped over.

"Are you quite sure, Allarand? I may not be familiar with her species, but this discoloration on her face-feathers does not look natural," the woman said.

"That's not a DISCOLORATION! That's BLOOD!" I roared with my actual voice, secure in the knowledge that all anyone but my master would hear was a series of hissing chirps, the whole bandwidth of which their ears couldn't pick up and which their brains couldn't translate.

"Quite sure, yes," Allarand nodded, then thought to me, 'Keep calm, Songbird. I'll have you fixed in no time. It will awe them and make your new enemies think twice about hurting you again.'

He put his hands on my face very gently. The cold metal felt glorious. Then my skin started to tingle. I knew the nanites he transferred to my cells were too small to feel, but still...

'You make it sound like I was looking for trouble. I assure you, Master, I had a smashing time talking to these kids before that rampaging crow came out of nowhere and started calling me names!'

'And, of course, you had to respond in kind.'

The heat in my face receded, and the headache got better. As did the back of my skull. Allarand bent down to touch my leg and back.

'Nooooo!'

'Do you even know what counts as an insult in this society?'

The kids' faces were pure wonder and delight as they watched me. I wished I could see what was happening. There was a strange sensation as something in the back of my head returned to its natural position. Now, even the high priestess seemed slightly impressed.

'I would guess "slave" is very high on that list.'

'You are mistaken. "Slave" is a state of being like "child" or "indisposed". It is not in itself considered a bad thing. It just is.'

'Didn't sound that way from what the crow said.'

My back made an ugly popping sound, but there had to be nanites blocking my pain receptors because I didn't feel anything. R'sal made a face, though.

'Some are more troubled about certain concepts than others.'

'How do you mean?'

Allarand gestured vaguely, then held out a handker-chief to me. I mumbled my thanks, took the thing, and turned around to watch my reflection dab away the blood pooling in the crevice between my beak and my cheek. The crack in the horn was brimming with silvery things moving, then hardening out as they found their places.

'The nanites will hold your beak together for now and aid your natural healing abilities,' Allarand's voice echoed in my head.

I studied the reflection of my master and the other people. The priestess and her entourage waited patiently and unphased. The crow's guards stood unnerved and stupefied. The kids still sported giant eyes. Except for whip-girl, who studied the high priestess. The Haslar crow clenched and unclenched her hands repeatedly in the folds of her robe. The paleness in her face had receded somewhat, only to be replaced by an uncertain uneasiness. She shared a short glance with whip-girl, which felt accusing. Whip-girl shrugged so lightly, I almost missed it.

'Are you quite done?' Allarand thought-asked, 'I feel obliged to tell you that it is considered an insult to keep the high priestess waiting.'

'Of course. I'm sorry, Master.'

# CHAPTER TEN

## THE BOY

"So, you ran away to get help," I whispered to R'sal when we boarded the transport shuttle to the temple. He nodded.

"That was very brave of you. And you have some mean skills in skedaddling."

"Ske...daddle...ing?"

"You know, like, running away."

"Oh," his shoulders drooped.

"You sound upset. I surmise skedaddling is not a valued trait in your culture?"

He shook his head.

"We Haslars are a strong people. We weed out the weak, so everyone else can thrive," the lady with the second most gems in her face said. She didn't look at me but the crow and whip-girl, who'd been seated next to each other and across from us.

"And how do you do that?"

"The ceremonies, of course."

After a moment of silence, the woman looked at me. Like I was an interesting specimen of some sort.

"You don't know about the ceremony you're here to witness," the way she said it, made it both question and statement, yet without any special emphasis. We could have been talking about the lack of weather on this planet.

"Well...," I stole a glance at Allarand, but he was deeply engrossed in a whispered conversation with the priestess, "No. What's it about?"

R'sal answered, "It's when we get our first stone! It marks a child's acceptance into society. ...or, well, you know... their end."

"Their end?" my gaze drifted to the rest of the kids and parents we'd picked up along the way. There were thirtysomething children. Most of them accompanied by what I assumed were their mothers.

"The stones keep our genetic code pure and strong. If a child is... corrupted, its body cannot accept one. The child dies," there was a short glance the woman stole at R'sal that made me pause.

"You kill the child?"

"No!" she shook her head, "We need the stones to activate our genetic code. We cannot live without at least one, and if one is not accepted..."

Her gaze drifted downward.

"...the body expires," R'sal finished.

"What? Don't you Haslars always brag about how advanced you are? Don't you have a cure for this?"

"This is not a disease!" the woman hissed, "This cannot be cured; it *should* not be cured! This is how our people ensure we stay as advanced as we are and do not mutate out of control, regressing into barbary and insignificance! We have stayed strong this way for thousands of rotations. Other races come and go, but we prevail. It may not be preferred by those who...," she faltered. R'sal took her hand, holding it firmly between his tiny fingers, "...are left behind, but it is inevitable."

I swallowed. The concept of a rite of passage wasn't new or horrifying to me. I myself had almost lost a hand when besting my first game.

But that had been a test of lessons learned and skills practiced. To just wait passively and see if your genes checked out seemed so... random and brutal for everyone involved.

And also, I felt like this made me much sadder than it had any right to. Maybe it was a remnant of what had happened to me, of that great depression I'd battled for so long. At this point, anyone losing their child seemed like an unbearably cruel whim of destiny.

*Strangely enough, this would never fade. If anything, encountering Humanity and pretending I was one of them made my feelings regarding this point line up even more with that of the average Human mother.*

*Back then, I just asked,* "And why do you think R'sal won't make it?"

The boy pulled at his shirt and showed me the lump on his shoulder I'd noticed before.

"There are signs hinting at genetic disruption," he shrugged, "But it's not final. It's just a hick-up, some injury I can't remember. I'll make it. I have to. I'll fly to the stars one day!"

"Yes, R'sal. Yes, you are," their gazes locked, and my heart broke for them. There was a light in their eyes like they'd agreed silently to believe for each other's sake, even though they both knew better.

I cleared my throat, "So, how many die and how many live?"

"One in six dies."

Well... those were actually pretty good odds. Especially considering that they were unlikely to lose many children to disease or nature.

Not like my girls and the uncounted others catching a deadly flu when the worst winter in recorded history had held half our planet in a relentless grip for months, when a sudden freeze foiled all attempts at keeping warm, and the crisp air and raging snow storms rendered any thought of flying for help useless. Those were the dangers of deciding to live without all that technology surrounding me right then on that Haslar world.

"What about her?" I asked, to get my mind off things, and pointed at the crow.

"Cu'Lar? If she survives this day, she will be punished severely. It might just be a problem that solves itself, though."

"How do you mean?"

"H'Gar'esh thinks my daughter won't make it either," the crow hissed, "But she's wrong! My daughter is worth ten of those bad apples she spawned!"

Whip-girl seemed ready to melt into her seat.

R'sal's mother answered as if the other Haslar didn't even exist, "Her daughter might not survive the ceremony. She's Cu'Lar's third child, and both her sibling were unworthy. If she dies too, the mother's genetic code must be unable to pass its strength to the next generation. In this case, Cu'Lar will have the choice to either die with her child or to take a slave gem. Most choose the gem these days."

"Most of us don't have a high family whose name they can defile with their bad seeds!"

R'sal tensed up, but his mother held him in his place.

"Well, 'most of us' is what's wrong with our people," H'Gar'esh looked at Cu'Lar directly for the first time since we boarded the transport, "Haslar like you are what makes us soft. If you would rather take the stone and become someone else's pet than admit your deficiency and die an honest death, you are a coward!"

A ghostly silence had taken hold of the other passengers as all eyes were on the two women. They stared each other down, but no one followed up verbally.

"So," I coughed, "A slave gem? What does that do?"

"It renders her sterile, pacifies her mind and body. She will be shipped to another planet to live out the rest of her life as a slave," H'Gar'esh answered without taking her gaze off Cu'Lar, who crossed her arms and leaned back.

"Haslars can be slaves?" I was dumbfounded. I'd never heard of that concept.

"Only to other Haslars. But yes, they can."

"What about the fathers?"

"The fathers are of no consequence. The mother's genes should be strong enough to prevail."

Copper-boy squeezed his mother's hand again.

The pieces of my heart could not find each other again. A horrible understanding dawned on me.

"Wait. How many children have you had before R'sal?"

# CHAPTER ELEVEN

## RITUAL BUTCHERY

'Master?'

'Yes, Songbird?'

'Is it really necessary that I attend this ritual? They obviously don't want me here, and I wouldn't want to be the reason for any resentment falling back on you because of what I represent in their eyes,' I looked straight ahead as we walked so as not to make my true intentions too obvious, 'Maybe I should just... wait outside?'

The guardian kept his place in the procession with liquid ease, like he'd done this a million times. With how old he was, he probably had... He'd probably seen this ugly ritual play out too often to truly care anymore.

But then, he'd stopped to save me, so ...who knew how much he actually cared for others?

*I still haven't made up my mind on this point even today. Back then, he'd already decided what would happen, of course.*

'No,' was all he said.

'Master, I—'

And he was far from taking my barkbeetle shit at face value.

'On average, only one in six dies,' his voice cut off my thought and echoed in my head, 'It is painless and quick. Besides, I thought you found their race to be too numerous in this galaxy.'

'These children have no chance to influence the outcome. This is not a rite of passage, it's butchery!' I retorted.

We passed under some decorative arcs as we marched deeper into the temple, then the floor turned into an ascending slope, the corridor spiraling higher and higher before us. There was lots of gold and sparkling stones and some giant, eerily lifelike statues, but I really didn't feel like admiring the artwork.

Right ahead, the priestess and R'sal's mother conversed in hushed voices.

"Please," the priestess murmured, "you would have a good place in my household."

"That would not be me in your household. You know this as much as I do," H'Gar'esh shook her head, "I understand. It would be hard for me to lose you too. But you should not seek to hold on to an empty vessel and tell yourself it was me."

The priestess's head dipped down a notch.

"I left detailed instructions with my assistant. Besides, everything will be fine. R'sal will make it, and there is no point in this discussion anyway."

It seemed to me that the other woman wanted to respond, but H'Gar'esh let herself fall back, putting Allarand and me between them. R'sal started to follow, but the priestess caught his hand and held it for a tense second.

The boy guided the back of her hand to his forehead and let it rest there for a moment.

"Until later," R'sal whispered. They let each other go.

I turned to Allarand to get my mind off things. I knew by now when trying to sway his opinion was a forlorn hope. He would drag me in to witness this thing, and any more attempts at evasion would be dishonorable, indeed. He was the master, and it was my place to shut up and deal with it.

'And why does the priestess want you here, anyhow? As I heard it, your kind is as seldomly seen in this part of the galaxy as anywhere else, especially not to witness something as "mundane" as a first stone ceremony,' I changed the subject.

'She had a question,' he replied.

'What was it?'

'She asked me for the likely outcome of this day.'

I remembered how he'd been formally introduced to R'sal and H'Gar'esh. How he'd held the boy's hand for a long moment.

'What is the likely outcome?' I wasn't sure I wanted to know.

He shook his head, 'This is her answer to know.'

---

The Star Chamber was aptly called, for it was the domed room I'd seen from that window back at the port. Its ceiling was so high a midsized shuttle could've done aerobatics in the rising sunlight. Steps lined the walls all around, occupied by more Haslars. Primarily women, I noticed, but there were also men and children—some barely older than the ones down here with us. Altogether, the crowd of spectators numbered in the lower hundreds.

This had to be a big chunk of the colony's inhabitants, if not most of them. As soon as the procession entered, everyone fell silent, stood, and placed their hands flat onto the center of their chest while they bowed. It was so well coordinated; it made me shudder with the creep factor of it.

'Why do they do that?' I asked Allarand.

'They show their respect to those who come before the trial and might die. Some might think of those they lost. To die here is considered a sacrifice preserving the purity of their race as a whole, and it behooves everyone attending to acknowledge this fact.'

'Mother! Haslars really are cold bastards.'

'That may be your opinion,' there was that smirk in his voice again.

'Right. Do we have to do something?'

'No. As observers, we are wise to not overly call attention to our presence.'

'That seems unlikely to work in this crowd,' I wanted to scratch myself, like, *everywhere*. All those black eyes made my feathers rise.

The high priestess took her place next to an ornately engraved table. It wasn't very large. Just big enough for a child of four or five rotations. Allarand stopped at the other end, at a respectful distance from the stone slab. Following his example, I positioned myself next to him but half a step farther back to indicate my function. The procession of children and parents had parted at the door, moving in both directions. They created a perfect circle, which only excluded the table ...and the hole. Some small distance from the table to its right, there was a hole in the ground, framed by ornamentations and burn marks. Was this where they disposed of the bodies?

'This is actually a marvel of technology,' Allarand said, 'Look up.'

I did. As did everyone. High above, several lenses of different colors and sizes clung to the ceiling like crystalline aphids. When the light of the passing sun hit the dome, they started to move silently on metal rings and gears. Cutting through the ghostly spectacle, the voice of the high priestess reminded her audience of the occasion and why this was so important to their people. Finally, the first lens caught the sun's rays, and, by being passed from one lens to the next, they were intensified into radiant brightness. A humming shield rose up from ground to ceiling, and when all the lenses lined up, one single beam of white-hot sunlight burned its way down inside a cylinder of crackling, Haslar-made energy.

'What you see are actually two energy fields,' Allarand explained, 'One on the outside, then a vacuum gap, then the other shield, then the sunbeam. If there were no vacuum between the beam and us, the sun would heat up this room and vaporize everyone in 1.3298 seconds.'

'1.3298 seconds, heh?'

'Give or take. Also, your eyes would burn out by looking at the sunlight directly if the lenses didn't filter out a partic-ular range of color.'

'Damn,' a shaking breath escaped my lungs, 'Where is all that energy going?'

'To the core. It will power this settlement for one rota-tion, until the sun reaches the right position to repeat the process.'

'So the ceremony is actually about reloading the battery?'

'Of course not. The ancient builders were just... multi-purpose-oriented.'

'Wait, you mean a local rotation, don't you?' I asked, after his nonchalant tone had really sunk in.

'No, a standard rotation,' his eyelights flickered barely noticeably as he glanced at me, 'Back in the day, the Ancients adjusted the rotations of all Haslar inhabited worlds so that they would correlate with the rotational shifts of the new homeworld. By now there may be minor deviations, but those are negligible. The deviation of this planet's rotation is about 1.2503 days.'

I blinked.

*MOTHER! Excuse me???*

'The Ancients adjusted the orbit of this planet because they wanted to enforce a standardized time calculation???' *how was such a thing even possible? How could one people shift an entire planet? Or several?*

Allarand indicated an indulgent shake of his head, 'It's not about the time calculation, it's to ensure that this ritual can be performed everywhere in time.'

For a few seconds I just stared at him, speechless. Finally I asked, 'When was this temple built?'

'About 15,329 standard rotations ago. This is a rather new installation.'

'DAMN!' my mind boggled at the idea of something that old. My people weren't that old, 'Wait, do THEY know how this works?'

Allarand smiled a small smile. He bowed when the high priestess acknowledged his presence as a great honor for the proceedings.

'Bow your head, eyes to the ground,' he instructed.

I followed his lead. The priestess nodded. I noticed her entourage had split up. Two of the men still stood behind her, one step to either side. The other two had positioned themselves in front of the closed doors.

"Let us begin," the priestess gestured. One of her servants produced a datapad, which looked very ceremonial with its gold engravings and sparkly case. The high priestess accepted the pad and read aloud, "T'shiff, first daughter to T'Hss. Please step forwards."

T'shiff was a scrawny little thing.

Her mother only had three stones herself, so I guess she didn't have much to feed and clothe the girl. Or herself. Both their ceremonial garb looked well-worn ...by someone else if the bad fit was any indication. Leaving the ring of people, they stepped up to the opposite side of the table. The girl tried to stand straight, fighting the slight shiver pervading her limbs.

"There is nothing to be afraid of, T'shiff," the priestess's voice wound itself around my heart like a soothing bandage. The girl and her mother took a visible breath and stopped fidgeting.

A green gem on the priestess's brow sparkled for a moment.

"Please choose a stone, Little One."

Servant number two stepped around the table and kneeled, so the girl could look into the box he presented her with. As could Allarand and I.

Warm sunlight bathed the crystalline material it was made of, and the hundreds of little gems contained within drank it up greedily, only to throw it out into the room again as a fountain of sparkling, multicolored incandescence.

"Wooooow...," I breathed.

The girl's tiny hand reached into the box, her fingertips browsing the stones. She paused for a second, moved on, paused.

"Take your time, T'shiff. One of them will sing to you. Choose that one," her mother said.

'What does that mean?' I thought-asked, 'Is it superstition, or can they actually feel some kind of connection to these things?'

'It is not superstition. Every stone unlocks a different genetic code. Not all Haslars have the same genes, though. So, if a stone fits their genes, they can feel it. It is a strange sensation. I believe you would liken it to touching a very low electric current.'

Nimble fingers closed around a blue stone, and after a last hesitant heartbeat, the girl fished it out, prompting the servant to close the box and retreat. The steps in front of the table didn't reach quite high enough, so her mother had to help T'shiff up. The girl lay down, holding the stone in her cupped hands like an offering.

With well-practiced efficiency, the priestess made a small incision in the girl's brow. Then she accepted the stone and placed it inside the wound. For a moment, nothing happened.

Everyone held their breath.

Or maybe that was just me. It was awfully quiet, though.

Allarand's eyes sparkled when I turned my gaze to him. He nodded in the girl's direction with his chin.

'Look.'

I didn't want to.

Around the stone, the blood started to boil. The cut widened to let the gem sink in until it was embedded about halfway. Then the skin closed around it, hardening, holding the stone firmly in place. Tears ran down the girl's face like small rivers. She didn't cry out, though.

Her mother, having retreated two reverend steps before, hastened back to her side to help her up. They hugged.

T'Shiff clung to her mother like a monkey, burying her face in the hollow of her neck.

The priestess followed up by saying how the girl had passed the ancient test of the stones and was now part of society and blah blah blah... After spouting some formulaic-sounding reply, T'Hss carried her child off.

The two of them didn't stand with the others again, though. They got to climb the first step, which until now had been empty, and be part of the audience. Part of society, I guessed. After all, the woman's status as a tried and proven member of her people had also been suspended for the duration of this test, hadn't it? If it had been her third and if the girl had died, the mother's status would have been revoked. Or considerably lowered? I still didn't get that part with the slave gem.

With the following four kids, the proceedings played out very similarly. Most got up onto the table by themselves since they were all bigger than T'Shiff. One of them let his gem slip, and the servant had to pick it up. It seemed to be considered bad luck or an embarrassment or something because people shook their heads and started whispering. The boy's skin turned a darker shade as he lay down. One girl just jumped up the table like a gymnast. She didn't need help from her father, and when she was done, she went up to her new place without looking back, her gait a tad shaky, her head held high. The audience loved her.

Then the first child died.

# CHAPTER TWELVE

## AN IMPORTANT QUESTION

He was a slight kid. His skin seemed less shiny than that of the others, and a small hump marred his back. Some gazes lowered with the knowledge of what they'd seen before. The woman accompanying him displayed the flexibility and grace of a cat predator. Black diamond eyes radiated cold distance as she hurried the boy to the table. He turned this way and that, but she had a firm grip on his shoulder and propelled him onward.

"I don't want to choose!" he squealed when the servant presented him with the box.

"If you don't, I will," the mother hissed, "We talked about this! It doesn't matter anyway, so do you want to fall ill and die a horrible, long death, or do you want it to be quick and painless?"

The boy looked down, tears streaming down his cheeks in silent rivulets.

"Choose, P'shik!"

The boy reached out with one trembling hand and took one of the stones without looking, without deliberation.

He pressed it to his chest, knuckles whitening as his mother picked him up and deposited him on the table.

"You're very brave," the high priestess said, stroking his cheek, "This will be quick. You need not be afraid."

The boy's shivers stopped, and he opened his hand to relinquish the crystal. A sudden glaze overlaying his eyes made my skin crawl with apprehension. The priestess made the incision and set the stone, a light purple one, in with gentle care. The mother kept her eyes on him the entire time. Her soul seemed a galaxy away, though.

'What exactly would happen if the boy hadn't chosen?' I thought-asked to get my mind off what was most likely to happen next.

'It is as she says. If the child did not come to get his stone, he would die regardless. It would be a painful and drawn-out process in which his genes would disintegrate and his body liquefy on the molecular level. His nerves would fire haphazardly and keep him in constant pain until he expired. It could take weeks. To make him take the stone is the kind thing to do. It is the only thing she is allowed to do.'

I clenched my fists and beak hard to keep them in line with my 'no trembling in front of Haslars'-policy. The all-knowing one's fingertips brushed the back of my hand. An outside observer might have seen an involuntary movement. I knew better. It wasn't proper protocol for a guardian/master to grasp some mortal's/servant's hand and hold it for support. Didn't mean he didn't mean to.

The boy P'shik closed his eyes. His blood began to boil like it had with the other children. Then there was a *crack*. A purple light flickered in the crystal, spraying sparks outward into the silvery liquid. The boil stopped. The boy blinked. Once. Twice. Then a shudder ran through the small frame. One last breath escaped his slightly parted lips. His eyes stopped moving. His chest didn't rise or fall anymore. There was only stillness. Utter, unnatural stillness. I caught a single tear shimmering in the mother's right eye when she picked up the empty shell and walked over to the beam of light.

The hum of contained energy was all one could hear. She gazed into the brightness, holding her son for a second longer before she flung the body in. One graceful movement of her petite frame and the boy passed through the force-fields and vanished into the light. The woman stood for a moment, watching the beam. Then she stepped aside to join the audience.

It had only been her first child, after all.

———

There were three more deaths conducted in respectful silence. All in all, 31 children lived and joined society.

The woman Cu'Lar and her daughter, whip-girl, stepped up. Even if I'd had the same speaking apparatus as them, I don't believe I could have pronounced the girl's real name if my life depended on it.

It didn't seem like a coincidence that those two were the second-to-last pair.

H'Gar'esh and R'sal being last. They stood so calm, one could have confused them with some of the nice statues of warriors and priestesses in the next room.

"Cu'Lar. This is your third child, is that correct?" the high priestess asked.

Cu'Lar nodded, "It is, Your Excellency."

"The other children did not live."

"This one will. She is strong!"

'What is it? What do you see?' Allarand's voice ghosted through my thoughts as they tried to form an accurate picture of what was only a vague apprehension, like too few puzzle pieces trying to build a picture in too large a frame.

'I'm not sure. I feel like something makes that girl very, very nervous. I mean, even for this situation, way too nervous.'

'She does not display open signs for more than the moderate level of stress this situation is bound to cause,' he kinda disagreed.

'I don't know what, but something is wrong. And the girl knows it.'

The guardian studied the child further while priestess and mother traded insults, veiled in formality. A sense of restlessness started to engulf parts of the audience as the proceedings veered off course.

Finally, Allarand nodded slightly.

"High Priestess," he interjected into a short pause in the conversation, which the women bridged by starting a starring contest. He bowed with the liquid ease of perfect understanding.

"Yes, Allarand. You may speak," the priestess reciprocated the gesture of respect.

"I would like to ask this girl a question."

Murmurs started in the crowd. The high priestess took a small step back like Allarand had just hit her. The girl blinked rapidly. The servants looked at the priestess. R'sal's mouth dropped open. H'Gar'esh's brows furrowed.

Cu'Lar was the first to speak.

"This is highly improper!" she squealed, "You cannot allow this!" she looked at the priestess, "This is a Haslar ceremony! He is here only to observe!"

The priestess nodded slowly, "This is true. Allarand, your request is out of order and quite unprecedented."

With another bow, the guardian explained, "I understand, High Priestess. However, my duty as part of the Great Neutrality is to gather knowledge so my race may further its insight into the universe. Sometimes, small things may have vital importance and can enlighten us about bigger contexts. Also, it is customary for all to answer my people's questions."

The priestess smiled, "That it is. You may ask your question."

"But—"

"Silence, Cu'Lar!"

Allarand closed the distance to the girl and kneeled, so their eyes were on the same level.

"Dear Child," he addressed her with the same respectful tone as he would the priestess, "As you well know, it is customary for units of the Great Neutrality to ask questions. For your honest answer to one of mine, you may ask one in return. You may ask me anything. Understand that I cannot answer all questions. Contrary to our title of respect, we are not all-knowing. If we were, there would be no point in asking, after all."

He gave the girl an easy smile, and she seemed to relax marginally.

I remembered how he'd given me that speech. The promise of knowledge could be very ...intimidating. Amidst the turmoil of life, the right question was hard to find. What was the one thing you just *had to know*? This was very different for each and every one of us, after all...

"Do you understand?"

Whip-girl nodded.

"This is my question then: How old are you, Child?"

As if he'd spoken some magic words, the girl stopped fidgeting and let out a breath.

Cu'Lar opened her mouth. In response to a sharp little gesture from his mistress, the guy with the box whacked that insufferable crow a good one. I heard bells ringing just by looking. It all went down silently; the girl never noticed. She gazed at her feet once, then back into Allarand's eyes.

"Four Rotations," she confessed.

R'sal's eyes widened. H'Gar'esh looked at Cu'Lar before anyone else did. People started whispering. The gems on both sides of the high priestess's face met in the middle, clinking together with the big one. It was the most melodic disapproval I'd ever witnessed. She snapped her fingers, and one of the servants picked up the dazed Cu'Lar and flung her onto the table like a rag doll.

"Explain!" the priestess hissed. A blue gem on her left brow began to glow with pulsing luminescence.

"No," Cu'Lar muttered. One of her gems activated in response. A yellow one. Everyone close to the table took a hasty step back as the brightness of the two stones increased.

"Insolence! You will bow to my authority!" the high priestess growled, closing her hand around the other's throat, "The records state that you had a child five rotations back. This one says she is only four. What happened to your third child? Was it malformed? Did you kill it?"

I couldn't look on; it was too bright. When I turned my head, shielding my eyes with my arm, I saw Allarand holding the girl's face to his chest and H'Gar'esh hugging R'sal to herself, both observing the scene unfolding, seemingly unperturbed by the radiance.

"I WILL NOT BOW!" Cu'Lar screamed, "I bowed all my life! I'm strong! As strong as you are! I deserve to live!"

"You deserve to be flogged for your deceit! Is this girl even your child?"

"Yes! Yes, she is! She's flawless and pure! Her genes are strong, just like mine!"

"So why would you risk her life by subjecting her to the Choosing one year early?" the priestess challenged.

"What choice do I have? I must present a child, don't I? I'm not like your idiot sister, who brings a deformed child to the table when her life is at stake!"

There was a crackling sound, very faint.

It was the sound a hollowed-out branch made when one put one's foot down on it, only to find it wasn't able to take the weight.

A choking sound followed. The priestess hissed something. Finally, a loud crack boomed through the hall. The yellow light blinked out. For a few heartbeats, everything was blue luminescence. I heard H'Gar'esh take two steps toward the table. I could see the bones in my arm as dark shapes in front of my closed eyelids, the quills of my feathers slim lines running all over them.

Then the light began to fade. In a matter of seconds, some random blue sparks dancing in my vision were all that remained of it.

Once my eyes managed to focus again, I saw H'Gar'esh, her right hand firmly on her sister's shoulder, her left soothing the clawing grip away from Cu'Lar's throat. Her sister's arm was ripped open by long nails, silvery blood running down in small rivulets.

The body on the table twitched in an almost random fashion. Cu'Lar's eyes remained open but unfocused. Her breathing sounded forced. Blood poured from where the yellow gem above her right eye had cracked. It was a clean split down the middle. The space had welled up with silver, flooding the hollow around her eye and dripping down the side of her face like silvery-black tears.

"This is not just," H'Gar'esh whispered, "It is not honorable."

Her sister held her gaze for a whopping five seconds before she turned away.

"Right," she agreed, "Child, come here."

Whip-girl seemed to want to crawl into Allarand and hide there. But then she glanced over at her mother's prone form and straightened herself. She stepped up to the opposite side of the table and bowed to the priestess.

"Do you know what happened to your sibling?"

"I only know what she told me, High Priestess. She said that my sister had been malformed and died very suddenly. She said that I was born soon after. She...," the girl wrung the hem of her tunic in her tiny hands, "She said she would kill me herself if I didn't come to get my stone one rotation early. She claimed she'd done it before. I... I think she killed my sister. I don't know, but I think she did. Please, High Priestess! Please don't kill me!"

The priestess shook her head gravely. Her eyes seemed drawn and uneasy, "This is not your doing, Child. You have nothing to fear. You will be sent to a suitable home and will return in one rotation's time to choose your first stone."

"Thank you so much, Your Excellency!" the girl bowed again.

The priestess nodded, "Allarand, Should you want to share your opinion of this situation, now is the time."

"It is a sad fact that behavior like this can be observed in your brethren from time to time," he allowed.

Allarand, diplomacy incorporated.

"So, considering what you have seen and heard, taking

your knowledge and experience into account, you believe this woman is guilty of killing her third child."

Allarand took his sweet time, studying Cu'Lar, the girl, and the high priestess thoroughly, before he informed, "I compute the likelihood of her killing the child outright and with intent at about 32 %, the likelihood of her killing the child by negligence at 46 %,—"

"Your definition of 'negligence'," the priestess interjected.

She made every question a statement, probably so as not to break the rule that maybe wasn't one, in any case. That everyone was only allowed to ask *one* important question. This was still a conversation, and Allarand would have answered her anyway.

*Looking back on it, I believe he would have told her even more in order to outweigh her later cooperation.*

*Besides, they were old acquaintances; who knew what debts had accumulated in that relationship over the years...*

"Not taking adequate care in preventing accidents, malnourishment, or illness, for example."

"Continue."

"...the likelihood of the child dying because of its corrupted genes or unrelated factors at 18 %, and the likelihood of someone else killing the child for the mother's sake at about 4 %."

Considering this, the priestess gazed into the distance. One of the servants stepped up to her, cleaning and bandaging her arm so unobtrusively that he might have been part of the background noise.

"High Priestess," H'Gar'esh interjected, "The sun is passing. You have to finish the ceremony."

The sisters' gazes locked for another long moment before the priestess looked at her nephew. Once again reminded of the unpleasant task, duty and position forced on her, the woman's head drooped ever so slightly.

"Yes. Of course," the priestess shook it off and stepped around the table to address her people.

"It is my judgment that this female, Cu'Lar, has caused the death of her third child because she found it deformed and unworthy. Since we cannot determine without further investigation if she killed it on purpose or by neglect, we will judge her on her other crimes first. She betrayed her priestess and her people by trying to deceive us, by bringing a child too young to receive her first stone to the table. She also attacked and injured the aide of a unit of the Great Neutrality, to whom I personally granted the hospitality and protection of our planet. And she attacked me, her high priestess, as all of you witnessed. Such blunt disobedience and disregard of the rules and traditions our people have lived by for millennia can only be met with the ultimate punishment!"

One snap of her fingers, and two of the servants moved next to the table to hold the still almost unconscious Cu'Lar down, while the priestess reached into her robes and produced a small case.

"Cu'Lar, do you understand your crime and punishment?" she asked as she stepped close to the table once more. While the other woman got very agitated, she was also still dazed, her movements sluggish and unfocused.

"Too bad," the high priestess whispered.

First ripping a jagged line into the middle of Cu'Lar's forehead with her fingernail, she opened the box and retrieved from it a large crystal in the form of a half-moon. No, I realized, there were small jagged teeth adorning the convex side. It was supposed to be a sun, at least half of one. Like it was shaded.

Cu'Lar screamed with defiance and rage. A renewed attempt at escape caused the muscles of the men holding her to bulge. The priestess grabbed her head, slammed it down, and then pressed the crystal into the wound. Cu'Lar's scream rose even higher, her song changing to desperation and sorrow. Then her blood boiled, her other jewels lost their luster, her body and voice fell silent.

And her eyes...

'Her eyes...,' I whispered in my head. 'They're... just ... empty. What did they do to her?'

The servants stepped back. The priestess looked Cu'Lar over, then nodded. One of the men took the woman by the hand.

"Come," he said.

And she did. She stood and let him lead her away. There was no expression on her face, in her gait, or in her demeanor... nothing. She was like an empty shell.

'It is called a slave gem. It takes away a Haslar's will, makes them pliant,' Allarand explained

'I heard of it. What ...what will they do with her?'

'She will be put to work, probably in a special factory or private household. Since with slaves from other races, there remains a chance of rebellion, Haslar slaves are deployed when absolute and unquestionable obedience is preferred. It is customary to ship people like her to other planets. This reduces the probability of people she knew to meet her and be ...upset.'

'How can... how can Haslars enslave half the galaxy when this is their worst punishment? When this is what they fear most and hide away and try not to see?'

'Interesting question,' Allarand noted, 'I will have to consider it at a later time.'

He turned suddenly, "Wait!"

The servant holding whip-girl's hand to lead her away froze instantly. With unease, his gaze jumped from the guardian to his mistress and back again. The high priestess didn't notice. She was giving hushed instructions to his colleague, who was taking away the mother, and Allarand's voice had been sharp but quiet.

For a second time, the all-knowing one knelt in front of the girl.

"Now, what is your question?" he asked as if nothing notable had happened since their conversation had been so rudely interrupted.

Whip-girl blinked. Once. Twice.

Then she held out her hand for him to examine, "How corrupt are my genes?"

She didn't flinch when he took it and stroked his long fingers over her golden skin.

"3.962 % of your genes are corrupt," he judged after a moment, "I suspect you will go very far if you stay as careful and cunning as you are now and choose wisely your stones, your friends, your allies, and your enemies."

She nodded gravely.

"Thank you, Honorable Guardian," she rested her hand flat on her chest, "For everything."

Allarand smiled and returned the gesture. Once he stood, the servant took the girl away. He made her stand in front of the first tier, with her back to the audience. Then remained next to her, at attention, like a bodyguard.

'3.962 %, that's very, very good, right?' I asked my master.

'The current Haslar queen has a corruption of 3.249 %.'

'Whip-girl could become queen? Is this gene-thing determining that? Doesn't the queen's daughter become the new queen?'

Something very akin to laughter ghosted through my head, 'The Haslar queen is sterile. When she feels strong enough, her second-in-command can try to kill the queen. If she succeeds, she then becomes queen.'

'And what do you have to do to become second-in-command?'

'You have to survive the stone that comes with the job and be good at it. Only 5.3 % of Haslar women are pure enough to survive its implantation. And while it grants great power, it also makes them sterile.'

Those Haslars were crazy bitches. Seriously, who lived like this? How could all of this have evolve naturally? But then, it didn't. The ancient Haslars recreated their people to this image when they'd been on the brink of extinction. Allarand had told me so.

'Hey, whatever happened to the ancients?' I asked.

'Later. It is time.'

Time for what?

I looked back at the table.

Oh, no...

# CHAPTER THIRTEEN

## A FATE CHOSEN

R'sal was sitting on the table, holding his mother's hands in his. She whispered something, and he gifted her a reassuring smile. Then he kissed her hands and released them. The servant offered him the box, and he took a long time to feel out the stones. He finally decided on a green one. When he lay down, the two sisters' gazes met. Something passed between them, but I couldn't decrypt the message.

The high priestess accepted the jewel and made the incision. Her hand seemed to tremble for the barest second before she breathed out and ever so gently pushed the stone in.

"I'll go to the stars," R'sal whispered to his mother, who nodded.

She held his hand in hers until it went limp. Both sisters bowed their heads. As did the servants. As did the audience.

H'Gar'esh lifted the body of her third child like it weight nothing. She stepped over to the sunbeam unhurriedly, staring into its blinding heart for a long moment.

Then her gaze tracked one final round around the room. Wherever she looked, people stood and placed both their hands on their chests, bowing deeply.

H'Gar'esh nodded appreciatively, pressing R'sal's body close, she stepped into the light and vanished.

It felt like an eternity went by before the high priestess spoke some flowery final words and released the old and new members of society. The tiers emptied themselves in graceful silence. Even the servants left.

Allarand and the priestess stood like rocks left over after the flood receded.

When we were alone, Allarand spoke first.

"I'm very sorry for your loss," he said.

The Priestess nodded in acknowledgment.

"As I am for yours," she replied, "It is unfortunate that you decided to leave so soon. We hardly had time to talk today."

"I understand, but it is an appropriate moment to go. Besides, it's not like I'll go away completely."

"No, parts of the Great Neutrality are never lost, they say."

He shook his head, "Some are harder to reach than others, that is all."

She looked at me. I felt like she was searching for an answer in my eyes, but not knowing the question, I couldn't provide it, "I hope you're worth his trust in you."

Since I had no clue what to say to that, I just bowed my head.

Her scrutiny shifted to the sky.

"You have another 17 minutes," she proclaimed, then turned and walked away.

"What was that all about?" I whispered.

"No matter," Allarand faced me, "What did you learn today?"

"Haslars have a fucked-up society."

The guardian looked at me intensely, as if he wanted to observe the individual neurons fire in my brain. Then he nodded, "Yes."

"But this is not the answer to my question, is it? This is not the greatest secret you know."

"No."

"So, can we go then, Master Allarand?"

"In about 12 minutes, 42 seconds. *First Female to fly in the open Sky*, I have scarcely seen anyone who is as observant and empathetic as you are. I believe you don't realize how rare a gift you possess. Today was a test. You passed. You have a choice now."

I was so stunned by his sudden directness, it took a moment for me to notice the change. We were walking towards the beam of light, but it wasn't me doing the walking. I wasn't in control of my limbs.

"Allarand, what is this?"

"You learned things today that no outsider may ever take away from this place."

Panic reared up inside me when the beam's light filled out my whole field of vision. I tried to run, to turn my head, to twitch. Nothing. My body didn't waver in its intention. It was that thing in my head! It had taken over my brain, steering me like a puppet!

"You're going to kill me!" I realized.

"Yes. I'm very sorry, but it is necessary and, at this point, inevitable."

"But... But you saved me!"

And I had offered my life to him freely. Some detached,

calculating part of my mind understood now the folly of giving myself away without clearly understanding the implications.

Tears sprang from my eyes unbidden, rolling down my cheeks. They turned to vapor before they could reach my chin. Heat sizzled on my feathers.

"Why?" I gasped. My skin felt dry and too tight. Like what I might have felt if I'd stayed longer in Father's view on that glorious day so long ago. Long before all the madness and the changes.

"Why are you doing this? I won't tell anyone, you know that! By the Mother, why did you make me come here if you had to kill me afterward?" a thought took flight in my head, "Hey! That's not fair! You can't just give me the answer and then kill me! You gave me the talk! You—"

"You asked me to show you the wonders of the universe. You asked me to tell you the greatest secret I know. This is it. These are place and time and circumstance to under-stand it. Now here is MY question."

We stopped and faced each other. The yellow lights of his eyes shimmered with intensity, even though they were dimmed drastically in relation to the sunbeam. His metallic skin flared like a miniature supernova.

"Do you want to shake off your mortal vessel and take this unit's place in the Great Neutrality, wandering the universe, learning and knowing all secrets, until you've had enough of that, or do you want me to tell you only this one, the greatest one, and die for knowing it?"

"This unit's place?" I repeated dumbly.

"Yes. I'm tired of walking the universe, of being connected but separate. I wish to join my sisters and brothers in the Great Core. You are young, curious, resilient. You were beaten. Haslar-sanctioned raiders took your child, killed your family, almost killed you. Still, you wept for their children's deaths today. You saw there was something wrong, even though you had no experience with what was happening. Even though you had minimal exposure to this species' bodily expressions. You recognized and honored H'Gar'esh's sacrifice in your heart. You are qualified and worthy."

He wanted to say more but stopped himself and just looked at me.

I stared back for a long moment.

"You understand now," he smiled.

"It's you," I whispered, "This is the secret! The greatest secret! The ancient Haslars remade their people. They invented all this, built all ...this," I gestured up at the mechanics distilling the sunbeam, the crystalline dome, the table, and the box filled with gems, "...and you," I touched his chest. It was burning hot, my fingertips sizzled, but I felt no pain, "That's where the ancients went. They created the Great Neutrality and its units. And then they just... uploaded an entire people into it?"

"Not everyone. We were tested. But yes, you are correct. We made room for our new people to thrive."

"And to ensure they didn't destroy themselves again, you stayed around. You babysit them!"

"We babysit everyone. We keep the universe in balance. We are like... gardeners, tending different beds of flowers. Sometimes, you must cut some of the plants down so that the others may get better access to the sun. Sometimes, you let them grow wild for a while; sometimes, you give them extra nourishment. It all depends."

"Knowledge is power. You steer the entire universe with your knowledge, answers, questions, and advice ...so that the Haslars stay in the center of it!?"

"Yes and no. We started with that, mainly trying to keep our children in check, so they could flourish. But the more we learned, the more we cared. We have augmented our ranks with gifted individuals from other peoples, like you, over the millennia. Now we care for the entire known universe. We found that there are other dangers out there, dangers of which even we know little. They move in the dark reaches of space, where the signal of the Great Neutrality is not strong enough to penetrate."

"You think something else might come here? That something might endanger your people? ...my people? ...all people? Like in that ancient war you told me about?"

"Maybe. Maybe not for a long time. Maybe never. It is hard to say. Either way, you have to make your decision now. If you become part of us, you can never be erased. Do you want to join us and live forever in the Great Neutrality, or do you wish to join your family in death? Meet them again in the next life?"

That's when I finally understood the depth of his earlier deception—and the benevolence of it.

That really was my grave I'd helped him close and sanctify. I just hadn't known it back then.

I hadn't known my wings would be all that was left of my body once Allarand was done with me.

My flesh buried in that grave was meant to be the spiritual gateway left open, an anchor for my soul, meant to create the option to return to my people after dying so far removed from my roots.

Oh, had I only known back then ...But, knowing me, I would still have asked what I asked.

"So, you already uploaded my mind, then? Everything I am went through that little box you embedded into my head? Where is it now? Where do I exist right now?"

"Right now, you are here, with me, avoiding the question. You have 5 minutes, 3 seconds left to decide."

So I thought about it. Did I want to stay with the people who'd spawned the people who paid the raiders that killed my family, with no boundaries between our souls, forever, or did I want to give in to that grief I kept buried deep down inside and become one with the stars?

I understood H'Gar'esh's decision then. Maybe it was easier for a mother to go with her child when she'd already lost two other after raising them with that boundless love she'd shown R'sal. Maybe honor had never been her motivation. Was I like her or like Cu'Lar, willing to break all the rules, step outside all the boundaries and demand my life at any cost to others? But then, this was about me, not about other people. Just me. And maybe the entire universe. I wasn't like either of them, I decided. I was me. I would always be me.

"Will it hurt?" I asked.

"Yes," he seemed saddened by that, "Pain is the price we pay for becoming all we can be."

I swallowed, giving it another few beats of my pounding heart.

"I'm afraid," I confessed.

Allarand nodded, "I understand. I will be your guide. I will be with you every step of the way."

I nodded, "Okay, then."

We turned. He offered me his hand. I took it, and together we walked forward into the light.

# CHAPTER FOURTEEN

## WANDERING THOUGHTS



"...do you agree, Ms. Baileywick?" Glen's voice cut through my musings and demanded immediate attention. It was gentle and accommodating while still retaining that steely core of authority.

I blinked several times as I quickly retraced the conversation my body had recorded, acutely aware of my captain's eyes lingering on my face while wearing an expectant expression in the well-worn lines of his.

Gosh, when had I started to phase out like this?

"Indeed," I agreed to our head engineer's assertions as I nodded in the dwarf's direction, "As Dr. Lustig rightly points out, the braces we put on the stress fractures are only a temporary measure, designed to make sure the structural damage doesn't get worse. They barely mitigate the damage, and they won't hold should we abuse the *Gateshot* any further. Until we can get it fixed, we'll have to avoid rapid maneuvers, like sudden acceleration or turning overly hard."

Glen nodded, the expression on his face changing slightly to depict unhappy concern, "I see."

These facts weren't new, the update merely confirming that the deep-seated damages his carelessness had produced couldn't be remedied by Lustig's genius, no matter how fervently any of us might wish it.

Nick nodded grimly as he leaned back, arms crossed. The former pilot turned first officer was quickly getting accustomed to his new, unexpected position and doing an excellent job at it.

Glen's emerald eyes lingered on mine for a moment longer, the amused glint dancing inside confirming that he'd very much noticed my sudden absentmindedness.

"Eve, do you mind staying a moment longer?" my captain asked once the meeting was dissolved and everyone prepared to leave. ...Most of them undoubtedly heading to bed, given the late hour.

I could hardly remember what a good long night of sleep felt like, as my new form didn't need any. Being a Human was very refreshing in that the faithful mimicry produced what was probably a close imitation of this other species' proclivity to rest and dream—even though it was also an enhanced version that barely let me close my eyes for more than four hours at a time.

"Of course not," with a smile, I sat back down in the chair directly to the left of his desk.

Glen used the time until everyone had filed out and the doors closed behind the exec staff to shrug out of his uniform jacket and hang it over the back of his chair.

Then he reached down to pull a bottle of scotch and two tumblers out of the lowest drawer of his desk cabinet.

I followed his example, relishing the relaxing feel of removing the stiff garment. I would have liked to slip out of my boots, too, but that would have been very unseemly.

Shoes... even after years in this other form, whose vulnerable feet very much demanded the extra protection, they somehow still seemed like an unnecessary accouterment to me.

"Are you okay?" he filled about 4 cl into each tumbler, then slid one over, "You seem somewhat ...unfocused these last few days."

"Thank you," I accepted the tumbler and lifted it to sniff the liquor inside, like I'd seen him do before, like he was doing now. My memories still clung fretfully to my mind, overlaying the current experience with a strange sense of leaving and losing home as well as returning there.

"I'm sorry," I shook my head, trying to dispel the lingering emotions, "What happened... I guess it just reminded me of a few things. It brought up some memories I'd rather forget."

"The sunbeam?" the slight tilt of his head telegraphed his wish to know more about that fragment of my mind he'd glimpsed when he'd pulled me out of my panic a few days ago and helped me save Konani from going critical.

I nodded. It was still a mystery to me how he'd managed it. The only halfway reasonable explanation was at the same time impossible, because it presupposed that he'd used his magic on me. And magic didn't work on guardians, everyone knew that.

"Will you ever tell me what that was about?" he held out his tumbler.

"Maybe some day...," I touched mine to his, and a soft

*clink* echoed through the silent office. Through what was the cockpit...

My eyes wandered unbidden to one of the corners, and a different layout came to life inside my head. Allarand sitting right there at the navigation console, his favorite spot.

Me, waking up in that new body in what was now Suzy's office.

All the pain of the rewrite between being burned as myself and being resurrected as this other person, with all these rules and guidelines deeply embedded into my brain, written onto my soul. All those accounts. All those checks and balances...

"I destroyed something that wasn't mine," I heard myself confess, "This shuttle isn't just some... communal property. It belonged to my ...," I wanted to say "master", but it didn't feel right anymore. I wanted to say "friend", but even though I felt like that was true most of the time, with my death still at the forefront of my thoughts, it seemed counterintuitive. I wanted to say "murderer", but that seemed too restrictive a term. All Human terms seemed too restrictive to capture what Allarand had been and still was to me. So, finally, I settled on the approximation I'd chosen to describe what I was supposed to be to Glen, "my guide's. He lived in this space for thousands of years. No one builds ships like these anymore. I'm not sure where I could get the part to fix it."

*Probably in Haslar space, if anywhere...*

Glen only nodded. It was enough to convey the shame he felt at his losing control, at what had come after. For some reason, I found I could read him so well most times, while other Humans would often leave me confused and unsure of their deeper feelings and intentions.

Belatedly, he blinked.

"Thousands of years?" my dialogue partner's eyes visibly widened.

I shook my head indulgently, my tone mild as I explained, "Very few races are as young as Humanity, Glen. But that's a topic for another day."

"Maybe for tomorrow, at breakfast?" his eyes were filled with the same curious light as mine had been so long ago.

"Maybe," I winked.

We just sat there for a while, sipping our drinks and thinking our own thoughts. The scotch was vibrant with taste, multi-layered, and smooth. A whole dimension of flavor distilled into this unassuming amber liquid. Fascinating.

Warmth spread throughout my gut.

"You enjoy food and drink, even though you don't need them," Glen conveyed his educated guess, the question only hinted at in the tone expertly crafted by his deep voice.

Deep, multi-layered, and smooth, like his scotch. Ripened by age. He could be quite the charmer if he felt like it, and I often found myself intrigued by the way he would bridge the gap of alien strangeness and make me almost feel at home in his company, now that we'd finally laid those tiring misconceptions we'd both held to rest.

It was ...enjoyable.

Leaving the pain behind, which our previous conflict had sparked within my programming, was also nice.

"Yes," I smiled, "Human tastes are so varied. I like it."

"Is it very different from where you come from?"

"Tastes are... simpler there," I tried to recall it, but the memories of the last meals on my home planet had long since become hazy. I could have used the Great Neutrality's databanks to access other wanderers' recollections of food and drink they'd enjoyed there in crystal-clear recordings spanning all available senses—even some I'd never had and some Humans couldn't fathom—, but that seemed ungenuine and beside the point, "On my original home planet, production methods are closer to nature, less refined in many instances."

Before Glen could dig deeper, I raised an eyebrow, asking, "So what is it you really wanted to talk to me about?"

My captain shook his head in self-mockery, "Am I that transparent?"

"I understand that you are honestly worried about my psyche and the impact recent events might have had on it," I confirmed, "And I very much appreciate your empathy. But you've also been looking for a quiet moment to talk to me since the burning. Is it something Rupert said?"

The ancients knew what ideas that pesky spirit had planted in Glen's head back in that elevator. GaSIn hadn't been able to record the conversation, undoubtedly foiled by the magic Rupert radiated.

"Aye," my captain nipped his drink, then settled back in his seat to tell me all about it, ending with, "So, since you said you could talk about it once he told me what he was, I figured maybe we could have that conversation now."

I gazed into my empty tumbler for a few seconds, biding my time as I considered what I'd just learned.

"Well, as far as I know and understand, he didn't lie to you," I finally evaded.

"But he didn't tell me the whole deal either," Glen picked up the bottle, and I held out my tumbler so he could refill it, "So you're still not allowed to talk about what he didn't say?!"

Sometimes it was scary how he seemed to look inside

my head like I was an open book. Most other people were so easily fooled... but not he. It was eerily intriguing.

I nodded, "Correct."

Glen filled up his own glass as he considered his following words carefully. In moments like these, he would lead with whatever questions he wanted answered most pressingly. As if he thought of words as a limited resource.

"So, rebirth is real?" was his final choice.

"Indeed it is," I enjoyed another taste before continuing, "Most other species know this, but how they deal with the knowledge can vary. For most, it doesn't take away from the limitations of one life, though, because we know that the person we are in one lifetime dies at the end of it. It is our soul that is reborn, stripped of all memories. The question of what remains of the person you are once you die is one of the greatest mysteries in the universe. It seems that souls evolve in some way through the experiences they rack up, but how and why when they can't remember the instances that made them grow in the first place remains highly debated."

In a thoughtful gesture, Glen slowly pulled out the tie from his hair, combing the shoulder-length red-white strands with his fingers several times before redoing the simple ponytail.

"But you retained the memories of your last life?"

"Yes, they were uploaded into the memory banks before I died."

"What about your soul, then?"

"It was integrated into the Great Neutrality," I shrugged, "I'm not sure anyone truly knows how this is done. My people use an ancient technique, but it's partly magic, so we don't understand how it works. It just does. Retaining our souls allows my kind to see and recognize magic, and only the restrictions put upon us by our core programming preclude us from using it."

"Will you live forever, then?" curiosity sparkled in his emerald eyes.

"I have the potential to," I acknowledged, "Though I could probably be deleted. With all the trouble I'm causing, that might happen."

"So you have no fear of death?"

What he was really questioning was my motivation, as he was trying to understand the behavior that might spring from such an existence and how it would impact him and our crew.

"Of course, I fear death," I shook my head, doing my best to ease his mind, "Every soul fears death. It's only natural. Besides, I swore to protect you, and if this body gets destroyed, my people will come for the shuttle. They won't care for the crew. They'll crack the *Gateshot* like a nut to get to it. So I'll do my damnedest to stay around and ensure that doesn't happen!"

The tension in his posture lessened considerably.

We drank in silence.

# CHAPTER FIFTEEN

## KNOWLEDGE AND RESPONSIBILITY

"I still don't fully understand why the Velorians can't know you're on board," Glen mused after a while.

"Because the bogeyman you can't see is the one you fear the most," a mischievous smirk jumped onto my lips almost too readily, "They don't see me as an individual but as part of my people. A tentacle the kraken uses to feel out the water. And while we're perfectly happy to let things evolve as they might, we're still bound to keep the balance. We're not enforcing anything; we're no leaders or generals. But giving the right knowledge to the right people at the right time can change the fate of the entire universe. That's why everyone wants to meet us—to get their questions answered. And it's also why we're feared by some. See, there are far more Humans than Velorians, but they do have the more advanced technology. If war broke out between your two species, it could end badly for both. My presence in this system is a bogeyman the Velorians don't want to disturb. Because they don't know how the Great Neutrality might react to whatever they are doing."

"This question business, what is that all about?"

"It's a tradition as old as my people. Basically, it's tit-for-tat," I gestured vaguely, "See, normally, we don't hide, we wander the universe openly, and everyone who wants to—which normally amounts to just plain everyone—can come up to us and ask us things. The saying goes that everyone gets one question, no matter who or what they are. Now, that will be indicated, of course. People use all these ritualistic ways to ensure we understand this is the big question they have. So they can ask us about the weather and make polite conversation beforehand, without fearing they might lose their one chance to gain whatever is most dear to their heart."

"The knowledge of the universe at your fingertips," Glen understood perfectly what I was saying, "That's like winning the lottery."

"Exactly. And given how few of us there are, it's about as likely. Of course, we can't answer all questions. We can't tell what we don't know, and certain knowledge would be too destabilizing to the recipient or their society if we provided it, so the balance forbids us from answering."

"So, for example, you couldn't provide a Human with knowledge of your species' technology?" Glen aimed to clarify.

I laughed, "We can't provide ANY species with that knowledge. It's too dangerous. It's why we get inscribed with all these restrictions, so we don't exploit the gap, so we'll keep to our programming, so we keep the balance."

He nodded thoughtfully, "So, tit-for-tat... that means you ask a question in return? That's how you gather all that knowledge you then safeguard?"

"Yes, a question or request of equal worth. That's how it works... under normal circumstances."

He raised one bushy eyebrow.

"I'm in undercover mode," I gestured at myself, "See, when people don't recognize what I am, then I don't have to answer their questions. But then, the Velorians didn't tell you anything about us, so that makes it kind of a moot point where Humans are concerned."

"And what about Velorians? You said they let you in, so why didn't you just ask them what they did with the Human women?"

The memory of my meeting with Primary Velorian Ambassador Thallamon stood out clearly in my mind as my thoughts lingered on it. Everything I remembered was so clear and crisp now, not like those hazy, uncertain wisps of barely kept impressions that had come before.

"By tradition, the other one gets to ask first," I heard myself explain, "Theoretically, we can ask first, but it's rude, and no one needs to answer our question unless they want their question answered. No Velorian I encountered in this system posed me a question. Not one! And when I asked the ambassador what his plans for Humanity were, he didn't answer. That was a huge red flag. As I said, people normally consider it a great honor and the chance of a lifetime to pose us questions."

I let him consider this as another comfortable silence settled between us.

Finally, Glen mused, "I know what you are. Does that mean I get to ask one of these big questions?"

Smiling mildly, I shook my head, "I'm your guide; you can ask me all the questions you want. That's what I'm here for—everyone who's part of the crew can. See, the balance can be kept by actions as well as words. Everyone who's part of this mission essentially pays with their valuable time, work, and expertise to access my knowledge ...in addition to the generous salary they're getting."

Similar to me serving Allarand. It had only been this most precious of secrets that demanded the ultimate sacrifice. Had I not asked to know it, he might have still taken me along... maybe. Questioning him about it had left me with the impression that he wasn't quite sure about this himself.

"Within reason, I guess?" Glen smiled as he sipped his drink.

"Naturally," I nodded.

"You didn't tell the exec staff about the question-bit."

I gestured vaguely, "Well, I feel like telling them that I'm an alien robot with intimate knowledge about what's on the other side of that gate was revelation enough for one day. Rivers has been taking every opportunity to ambush and question me as it is..."

Dark laughter rose from his chest, smoothly filling his office with the outward expression of an amusement both of us felt inside, and I gladly joined in.

"So, to come back to the Velorians and your status as the bogeyman," Glen shook his head, "Won't they suspect you're aboard this strange prototype by now?"

"Most certainly," I acknowledged, "But they can't be sure. Short of actually making my presence known, I can't influence their perception in a definite way. I set in motion several 'sightings' on different planets to throw them off. With any luck, that's enough to keep them from doing anything radical while we're away."

Glen nodded, his eyes mirroring my concern, his spine straightening.

By the balance, Humans were marvelous creatures. While their bodies seemed so vulnerable and were destroyed so easily, they were also remarkably adaptive, fierce, and unyielding. Maybe it was their technological inferiority that had first made my heart go out to them. Perhaps it was their nature that had enamored me to stay and put on the line everything I was and could be.

A twinge raced up my back, an echo of the explosion tearing away my right-side wings, which had made me fall, which had killed me. It had forced me down this path I now found myself on, made me suspect similarities between the Velorians' conduct towards the Humans and the slave raids on my own planet. The only survivor of my village, of what had once constituted my whole world, I wished this on no one. I would make sure this didn't happen to Glen and his people.

Whatever the Velorians were doing with the women they lured away, probably even bought and kidnapped, I would find out. I would bring them back.

I would do for them what I hadn't been able to do for my own. What I was now explicitly forbidden to do for my son. Because my old life was supposed to be just that. My old life, unconnected to this new existence.

Had that ever worked for anyone, I wondered?

How long had it taken Allarand to truly leave behind what he hadn't been allowed to take along so many millennia ago?

"Glen, my body might be more durable than yours, but our souls are equally immortal. And just like you, I can't go back in time, no matter how much I might wish it," I laid my hand atop his and squeezed, "I can only go forward. That's all any of us can do."

Suddenly and without warning, his right hand jerked. He didn't hide it from me like he did with the rest of the crew; he knew that I already knew.

"You have nerve damage in your middle and ring finger," I stated.

Glen nodded as he started massaging one hand with the other. It probably helped with the stiffness, but employing only one hand was suboptimal.

I reached out in an offering manner. After a second of uncertainty, he let me take over, "I... might be able to fix that for you. Should you allow it."

"How?" he seemed cautious, "Dr. Fox said a treatment would be very difficult and time-consuming. She wasn't sure if she could fix it without replacing them entirely ...I've gotten through 96 years and a war without needing to exchange anything. I'm not too fond of starting now."

"So you finally consulted her?"

"Aye. She seemed surprised. Almost ...taken aback," Glen furrowed his brow, "I'm not sure why. But it was very strange..."

"Maybe it's because of your reputation," I shrugged, gently smoothing out the muscle strands underneath the well-worn, calloused skin. A lowering in his pulse indicated that he enjoyed the treatment, even though he was careful not to show it on his face.

"Maybe. So how would you do it?"

He knew, of course, just wanted to make sure.

"I would inject you with parts of me. They would link up to the damaged areas and repair them on a cellular level."

"Nanites?"

"Yes, nanites."

"If you can …repair people just like that," Glen raised a bushy eyebrow in unspoken challenge, "Why haven't you done it before?"

"I can't just repair everyone. I'm not allowed," I shook my head, "But you're my…"

I stopped myself, looking up self-consciously to find his gaze on me.

"Your what?" there was something blazing deep in those emerald eyes, daring me to say, not just think it, "If you're my guide, then what does that make me in your people's eyes?"

"My pupil," I admitted.

"Your pupil?" Glen burst into merry laughter once more. Like it was an absurd notion that he, with his 96 years of age, could be a pupil to anyone. Let alone bumbling old impostor me.

After a few seconds, I joined in again.

Sure, people everywhere beyond the Space Gate would have called his conduct highly disrespectful, and others of my kind would probably have felt slighted and been utterly dismayed, even angry. Just like I'd thought I ought to behave until mere days ago. Not anymore.

I could have fluffed up my now proverbial feathers and reminded him that the access to the well of knowledge I held was a tremendous gift he should be thankful for.

But he knew that, and he was.

I could have emphasized the age discrepancy between my Human disguise and my actual self, explaining that, given the strange nature of relativity and how time was measured differently from planet to planet, all things being equal, he didn't even have a whole Human decade on me.

But that would have been pointless.

Besides, I enjoyed the relaxed conduct we'd arrived at and didn't feel like proving anything to him anymore. And there was so much I could learn from him too.

When he was done expressing his amusement, Glen asked, "So why don't you help Suzy with her injuries? She's your pupil too."

"She has been cared for perfectly well. All she needs to heal up is time," I sighed, "You, however..."

I lifted his hand, studying it intently.

"What do you see?" interest brushed away the last remnants of his mirth.

"Your muscles, your bones," I brushed over his skin, following what lay underneath with my finger, "your blood vessels, your nerves. There. You have a bad spot there, very small. And another one here. And here. Probably the result of an injury or an inflammation long since healed. It hardened up your flesh, like scar tissue. I think fluid builds up there and presses on the nerves now and again, causing the misfires. I would loosen up the scar tissue and reconnect any nerves that are damaged. If you allow me to."

*If you trust me enough to let an alien robot inject you with nanites that could do whatever to you...*

I remembered the sunbeam. I remembered the feeling of being a puppet. I knew now how specific Allarand had planned that moment, how fine a line he'd walked to stay within the confines of our rules.

But Glen couldn't know all that. He couldn't know I wasn't allowed and probably not even skilled enough to do anything like that to him.

My captain took back his hand, took a moment to think, then a large swig of his drink.

"I'm sorry," he finally said, "But I'm not there yet."

"I understand," I knew by now not to push him, "My offer stands should you ever change your mind."

He nodded thankfully, then filled our glasses for the third time.

# CHAPTER SIXTEEN

## PAST AND PRESENT

When I left Glen's office an hour later, a slight buzz had crept into me, leadening my limbs while lightening my spirit. I couldn't actually get drunk and lose my facility for critical thought. What I experienced was just the part my body allowed so I could better understand and mimic the effect on my disguise. I could dial it back any time I felt like it, which mooted the point of getting drunk in the first place.

'Bummer,' as Suzy would say...

The fun-loving feeling did give me the impetus to walk into my own office, though, over to the back wall.

I willed the holo-field to shut off, so I may look at the display cases set into the wall. Of differing sizes, they were only ten centimeters deep so as not to make it too obvious to anyone standing next to it that the wall wasn't exactly located where one's eyes reported it to be.

One held the most recent editions to my collection: the necklace Ebbon had gifted me and the bracelet I'd won from him, placed another fateful bet on, and which Thea Robbins had duly returned to me the same evening.

There were a few other items I'd collected in Human space, but the ones I was looking for had been set up right in the center.

My eyes lingered on the small circles meant to be worn on one's foot talons, almost large enough to serve as bracelets to my current form. One for each chick I'd hatched, one for my mate.

The sorrow in my heart was muted and distant now, as was the itch to fly. I did indulge in the latter now and again when there was time and privacy. It didn't feel like some life-essential necessity anymore, just like good fun. I'd learned the trick of hovering in that air years ago, after carefully considering the movements with all the knowledge and understanding now at my disposal.

What I was looking for this evening was one showcase over.

I stared at the three larger rings made of pliable dark metal, normally worn around the upper arm, and studied the rows and rows of names inscribed on them. Students of their craft become masters, to then pass on the ring, so someone new may add their name to the list. My name was last on all of them—three loose ends in what should have been neverending lines.

I'd busted my tail feathers to become a warrior, had advanced up to third level, but never felt ready to have a student.

Not until now, anyway.

Well... there were many days I still didn't feel comfortable taking on that responsibility.

But Allarand persisted in stressing that this was normal. Saying it was a sign of a good teacher to realize they would never know everything and would always stay a student also.

And even though I wasn't a Karrkuishian anymore, even though I wasn't officially allowed to think like one, so it wouldn't influence my neutrality, even though this wasn't anything like the apprenticeships I'd gone through, and even though I felt more at home in the Human body than I did in any other at this point, I perceived the sudden need to link my past with my present.

The transparent case slid aside as I reached out to take the third-level ring. My eyes quickly found the last entry.

For a heartbeat, the sharp metal claw hovered over the ring.

Then I scratched *his* name right beside mine.

*Glen Michael MacAllister*

And replaced the ring in the showcase.

The holo-field sprang back to life as I turned to leave Allarand's shuttle, my mind already searching the cameras and sensors to find an empty hangar.

I felt like flying for a while.

~ *the end?* ~

Dear Reader,

Thank you for taking the time to read my book.
I hope you enjoyed it!

If so, it would help me enormously if you
leave a quick review on Amazon, so that other
readers discover this series! 😊

If you want to know how Nick and Gabe met,
sign up for my newsletter and get the novella
"Spartan Roulette" for free for Kindle,
other e-readers, and as .pdf-file!

Also, feel free to write me about what I can
do better, or just say "hi" at
Hi@KimNexus.com.


Yours sincerely,


Kim Nexus

# ACKNOWLEDGEMENTS (KINDA)

Even after publishing three books, it feels weird to write acknowledgments. Like I'm still some sort of impostor and don't deserve to. Also, as a self-publisher doing most of this stuff myself, there's hardly anyone else involved.

But I would like to take the chance to thank my dear friend and cover artist Björn, to whom this book is dedicated.

Thank you for sticking with me for over twenty years and not giving up on me even when I bludgeoned you with my overzealous honesty so severely that one time!

Thank you for always being a good sport, especially when I didn't deserve it!

Thank you for saving book 02's cover!

Thank you for taking a chance on the improved me and agreeing to become a business partner as well as a friend!

And last but not least, thank you for always putting in so much more effort than I could ever pay you for! I really do appreciate it!

The other person I'm insanely thankful for is my wonderful husband and editor, Jim, who's the greatest gift this life has ever granted me. Thank you so much for sticking with me, helping (and, if I need it, shoving) me along, and putting so much time and effort into this creative dream of mine. You're the bomb!

Also, big thanks to my beautiful kids for sharing me with this whole other universe, even when they would rather have me for themselves.

# HI THERE, I'M KIM NEXUS!

Welcome to my witching world!

I'm a full-time working mom living in Germany with my beautiful family in a house where each room is designed differently, because we hate boring things.

I'd love to read more than I ever get around to (especially more fiction), and when I do get around to it, I mostly enjoy paranormal romance and science fantasy.

Other interests of mine I always strive to learn more about are learning itself, self-betterment, motivation, bio-hacking, history and the English language.

Find out more about me at KimNexus.com or join my newsletter at KimNexus.com/Newsletter.

## Please Review This book!

I know, I know, everyone says it these days, but it REALLY DOES help us Indies out if you take just five minutes out of your busy day and quickly jot down a few impressions.

Tell the community what you liked and what didn't jive, so other readers know if this is the book for them and so that I can make the next one better FOR ALL OF US.

# Thank you so much!

See whole series
  & review on Amazon:

Say Hello 

I won't promise anything, since I do have a full calendar, like, all the time now, but if you have questions, suggestions, or found typos and the like, why don't you shoot me an email at hi@kimnexus.com.

  Or find me on twitter (twitter.com/kim_nexus).

**GET SPARTAN ROULETTE HERE:**

*"What of you? Do you think us dangerous? Is that what you will tell your captain?"* Federov challenged.

*"I don't need to,"* Felicity replied with a dry laugh, unwilling to show her fear, *"A blind fool can see that you are dangerous. The only question is, to whom?"*

~

I'm Lieutenant Senior Class Sergey Fedorov.

Tasked with a very delicate retrieval mission by Plutonian Command, accompanied by 60 of the most vicious commando troops our military has to offer and a reverent priest eager to join for no apparent reason, I find myself stranded in the void.

Saved by a curious ship of shady origin, we now depend on our hosts to ferry us to our destination.

For their cooperation we are authorized to offer our protection.

Given the enormous bullseye on their back, they sorely need it.

Well, at least their doctor is cute.

~

*Say, Witch Way to the Void?*

Witch Way Chronicles #04 - **WITCH WAY TO THE VOID**

is now available on Amazon

as e-book and print-on-demand!

# ALL BOOKS IN THIS SERIES

WWC #01 – WITCH WAY TO SPACE

WWC #02 – WITCH WAY TO JUPITER

WWC #03 – WITCH WAY TO SPACEDUST

WWC #04 – WITCH WAY TO THE VOID

# WWC #00 – SPARTAN ROULETTE
# (WWC SHORT #01)

# WWC #03.5 – SUNBURNT
# (WWC SHORT #02)

Sunburnt (*Witch Way Chronicles* #03.5) by Kim Nexus

---

Author & Coverdesign: Kim Nexus; c/o Block Services; Stuttgarter Str. 106; 70736 Fellbach

Developmental Editor: Jim Nexus

Coverart: Björn Frost [Give him some love at deviantart or instagram!]

Print: Amazon EU S.à r.l. (For executing print-on-demand center see identification on the last page)

---




ISBN-13 (paperback): 978-3-949552-18-2

ISBN-13 (hardcover): 978-3-949552-17-5